Teevichirikkunnavarkku
Vendiyulla Oppees

OXFORD NOVELLAS

Encompassing literature, popular and genre fiction, writers old and new, this series presents an orchestra of Indic voices

Series Editor: Mini Krishnan

Other titles in the Series

Vaadivaasal (Tamil)
   C.S. Chellappa

Tyanantar (Marathi)
   Saniya

Sheet Sahasik Hemantolok (Bengali)
   Nabaneeta Dev Sen

Dweepa (Kannada)
   Na. D'Souza

Moogavani Pillanagrovi (Telugu)
   Kesava Reddy

OXFORD
UNIVERSITY PRESS

Oxford University Press is a department of the University of Oxford.
It furthers the University's objective of excellence in research,scholarship,
and education by publishing worldwide. Oxford is a registered trademark of
Oxford University Press in the UK and in certain other countries

Published in India by
Oxford University Press
YMCA Library Building, 1 Jai Singh Road, New Delhi 110 001, India

ISBN-13: 978-0-19-809746-4
ISBN-10: 0-19-809746-8

Typeset in Berling LT Std 10/15.5,
at MAP Systems, Bengaluru 560 082, India
Printed and bound in India by Repro India Ltd

Jeevichirikkunnavarkku Vendiyulla Oppees
Requiem for the Living

Johny Miranda

Translated from Malayalam by
Sajai Jose

OXFORD
UNIVERSITY PRESS

To
my mother
Helen Jose

CONTENTS

Series Editor's Note

> 'Freedom is knowing and understanding things
> quite other than ourselves.'
>
> —Anonymous

Writers have always experimented with forms in their search for the best vehicles for their thoughts, moods, and words. While there might be arguments about what length defines the genre, the novella was shaped and recognized in the late nineteenth century as allowing for greater development of theme and character than a short story without being burdened with the demands of a full-length novel.

Our broad goal in assembling the Oxford Novellas, a unique series combining substance and brevity, is to present the least studied genre from one of the world's oldest literary traditions which includes one of the most sophisticated pre-modern poetic theories. At a time when news is entertainment and literature has to compete with popular fiction, two criteria have guided our selections: socially relevant themes for readers who might want to know things quite outside their experience and understanding, and literary excellence. Thus, famous names march with writers few people have even heard of.

Having absorbed words from nearly four hundred languages, English is opulently equipped to interpret and express the cultural energy of the regions it once entered as the colonizer's voice. If, to paraphrase Wittgenstein, the limits of our language mark the limits of our world, we hope, from time to time, through this series, to move the borders of literary enjoyment further and ever further. Translation into English brings together the creative potential of different Indian languages, the special understanding of the world each one of those languages has, and consequently, the distinctive way they carry the memories and histories of those who use them.

The art of story-telling and the art of narration mingle to give us a literary mosaic made possible by translators working to move texts originally written in other languages into English. We believe that the translator is not merely an echo or a shadow, a reflection or a crib, but a fresh, strong supporting voice that conveys both the said and the equally vital 'unsaid' parts of the original into the receiving language.

MINI KRISHNAN

Author's Note

An oppees is a prayer for the dead. This novella tells the story of a people who are eligible for an oppees in every way, while yet alive.

It captures the life of the Anglo-Indian Latin Catholics of central Kerala, who have lived through great historical, political, and social upheavals.

They are not the same as those familiar characters in films and literature labelled 'Anglo-Indian'.

To this day, portrayals of Anglo-Indian lives appear as if cast from the same mould, with the same mix of prejudice, fantasy, and grotesque imitation. This novella is an exception. They may lack a firm grasp of their own history and ancestry, but they continue to live with the sense of isolation and conflicted identity that comes along with being a hybrid race; a condition which affects the very rhythm of their lives. They may call themselves Anglo-Indian and carry outlandish surnames that stick out like tails, but the fact is that the majority of them remain backward and poor. Western influences and the urge to display one's own culture before other communities have turned their men into spendthrifts and alcoholics. In comparison, the women tend to be thrifty and forward-looking.

Life for the coastal people of Kochi is but a passionate commingling with rituals and customs.

Life and custom on this coast is fertile and diverse enough to tempt any writer.

The influence of Christianity and the Church on these people is astounding. It would be impossible to describe their lives and not mention their religious rituals and practices. If it did not require any research or even effort for me to portray the essential strangeness of life here, with its innate magical realism, it is only because I grew up here as one of them.

In a time when people everywhere tend to speak alike and live alike, I consider it my good fortune to be able to record, through my writing, a unique way of living and speaking that is being lost. And yet, the purpose of the art form that is the novella is not the documentation of a society, or a description of its way of life and its customs and rituals. To do that, a historian or an essayist would more than suffice. In fact, they would be far more qualified to do it than a writer of fiction.

These are but mere ingredients in the writer's effort to create a fresh flavour in fiction, a completely original artistic experience. If it does not create the experience of delight that is art, then all page-stuffing that goes by the name of novel-writing is but in vain.

The writer is someone who, working in solitude and beyond the dictates of reason, weaves a peculiar 'pattern', in a way that only he can.

When elementary substances come together at a certain temperature and under certain conditions, knowingly or unknowingly, that pattern springs forth like destiny or revelation, much like how life itself would have germinated in primeval times.

What might happen if you add the wrong measure of salt or spice while preparing a dish can happen here too.

To the writer, the human condition, the material world, and people themselves are what colours are to the painter; no more. When you make choices that ignore this fact, you produce work that fails to create the experience of art.

***

Just like how every man and worm has a destiny, every book does too. Or so it seems to me sometimes. How else could a publisher as venerable and prestigious as Oxford University Press have got hold of this book, when no such thought crossed my mind, and when I did not make even the slightest effort in that direction?

The book's journey started in 2004, when it was first published in Malayalam by Mathrubhumi Books.

I had not met Sajai, the translator of this book, before he had decided to take up this work. Not only had I not been acquainted with Sajai, who grew up in Kottayam and now works in Bengaluru, but we had very little in common culturally.

Having read the book by chance, he came looking for me in a state of excitement. He took the rights from me, and went on to translate it as if possessed by the book. Even during that period of waiting as we searched for a publisher, I had only wanted to see it printed in English, it didn't matter by whom.

But Sajai's faith in the book, and his hopes for its future, were greater than that of the writer himself.

I bow before that generosity of faith!

***

Most books have, in their initial pages, an acknowledgement note thanking those who helped in its writing and publication. When this book was first published, it too had such a note. One of the names it mentioned was that of my dear friend Maju Thomas.

He is not with us anymore. Around noontime on 27 November 2007, he put an end to his life and departed for another world.

When I had met him the previous evening, he was humming the lines of a poem about death. 'I've had enough, I don't want to live anymore. I'm ending it,' he told me. He would not consider my remonstrations. Just before his death, he had watched a Malayalam film on television that depicted a suicide by hanging. When they found him dead and turned off the TV, the film was still going on.

The black spectacle of art taking a life!

Thirteen years younger to me, Maju had little connection with literature. Still, he would come and sit by me as I wrote, and read the manuscript pages on which the ink had not yet dried. The first reader of everything I wrote in those days!

Someone who loved good books, Maju would give his opinions freely, with none of the presumptions of a scholar or critic. I would appreciate his sincere and intelligent comments.

Maju could not leave anything behind that would keep his memory alive on earth. His soul must be seeing everything.... Let this note be a memorial to Maju!

May his soul rest in peace.

***

The stories and legends narrated by my mother who grew up in a village; her forcing me to attend the rites in church against my wishes; Pappa, who would subscribe to a great many periodicals at home even though we were perpetually short of money – all these served my writing greatly.

***

It was from my wife Blessy's stories that I got the fine and varied ingredients for making a character as proud, noble, aristocratic, and wise as Juana Mammanji. When the life and peculiarities of Blessy's own Mamma and those of many Mammanjis who lived in different periods came together in different measures, Juana Mammanji was born.

***

Finally, my gratitude to O.K. Johny of Matrubhumi, who took the initiative to publish the book in Malayalam; C. Radhakrishnan, who wrote the preface for the Malayalam edition; P.F. Mathews, who inspires and encourages me to write in new ways; my editor Mini Krishnan; and J. Devika, who wrote the enduring Introduction.

JOHNY MIRANDA

Translator's Note

In his preface to the Malayalam edition of *Oppees*, the writer C. Radhakrishnan likens the author of this short novella to a fish that lies still at the bottom of a muddy pond, observing the goings on carefully while remaining unnoticed itself. The analogy is apt for its protagonist Osha; it is through his all-seeing, unblinking – at times morbid – fish-eyes that the story is told.

The book has much more to recommend it, as I discovered later, but it is this distinct narrative voice – as if that of a ghost – that gripped me when I first read it. Others I thrust the book on to, were equally taken by it ('It reads like a revelation', was my cousin Vineeth's dazed reaction). I was attempting to translate bits of Malayalam prose into English at the time, and given its brevity and its simple style, *Oppees* suggested itself as a natural choice.

The author Johny Miranda was happy to give me the rights, but only when I got down to the task did I realize that the book's length was as deceptive as its simplicity. Mirinda's idiosyncratic style masks a highly compressed narrative, which – the confessional tone apart – holds its secrets close, like Osha's own occult village, one that is 'crisscrossed by canals, and ... run over by bushes'.

Being a novice at translation, I had only the original text for a guide, and therefore decided that the first rendering should be literal and as faithful to the Malayalam as possible, which could then be reworked to suit the English reader. This is, in fact, how it was done, and I hope the results are satifactory.

In many ways, the world described in the novella is unfamiliar even to readers of the original Malayalam. It's likely that they missed the significance, or even meaning, of many of the extremely local references, as I did when I read it first. In this version, I have tried to capture these separately in the glossary, so that readers who just want to get on with the story needn't be distracted. They point to fascinating aspects of Creole culture in Kochi, and the history of Kerala at large, and researching this was the most enjoyable part of my work.

I wish to thank my friend Gens George, who suggested the title; the library staff at Dharmaram College in Bengaluru, who allow me to use their resources without any fuss; editor Mini Krishnan, for her painstaking readings of the many drafts and her valuable suggestions; and above all, Johny Chettan, whose calm and genial ways provided a favourable climate for the work throughout.

SAJAI JOSE

Introduction

The Delicate Task of Recovering Cochin-Creole: Johny Miranda's *Requiem for the Living*

Fabulous Past, Lost Histories

Malayalees, the people of Kerala, love to nurture self-images. Our favourite self-portrait is the one which has the extraordinary mix of cultural flavours of our coastal cities as the background. It has an exotic touch; it throws soft light on the long history of our participation in the Indian Ocean trade before and after colonialism. We are unlike India, we often boast – we have been open to the world. Or even: we have been modern, in a sense, *at all times*. We have recast this image in ever-newer forms, always gathering congratulations in the end – the latest reinvention being at the recently concluded Biennale in Kochi, projected now as the ancient port, the fabled Muziris, where all the wealth of the world once arrived. We have also caught the imagination of scholars who seek to reshape us in even more exotic ways. Witness, for example, Ashis Nandy's views on Cochin as exemplifying a non-Eurocentric cosmopolitanism.

It has indeed been convenient for us to not look closely or critically enough at our fabulous past. After all, this image is one of the cornerstones of Malayalee exceptionalism vis-à-vis the rest of India. This has suited our admirers as well. We, and most of our admirers, have chosen to ignore the fact that this vision of tolerance was built on a society organized hierarchically as caste groups. In the framework of such a society, foreigners and foreign ideas were welcomed only insofar as they were willing to be integrated within the terms of the highly iniquitous hierarchy of caste overseen by the Hindu rulers of medieval Kerala. As early as 1507, the Kolathiri, the ruler of a principality in north Kerala, wrote to the King of Portugal that

> ... certain people who I and my Nairs [the upper caste which served the feudal elite] have as slaves and belong to the two castes, viz., the Tines [Tiyya] and the Mucoas

[Mukkuva – fisherfolk] should not be made Christians …
For with the conversion of these slaves, conflict may arise
between our vassals and these people. The Nairs derive
their income from them and they do not want to lose it'.
(John 1981: 347)

Not only does the narrative of local tolerance
conceal upper-caste Hindu elitism in shaping such
'cosmopolitanism', it also directs us mostly to look
longingly at the West. In other words, it makes us blind
to the historical shaping of this region as a 'cusp culture'
(a term coined by the sociologist Satish Deshpande), a
place which was shaped by both Western and Eastern
cultures. Whenever we speak of the East, we usually
refer to China. But rarely do we consider the possibility
that the references to 'Chinese influences' might have
a broader connotation including the many South-east
Asian cultures.

A major consequence of the above self-image has
been the relative invisibility of the hybrid communities
on the coast. Over the centuries, there have been several
references to mixed communities besides the better-
known Eurasians, called variously as *Topasses*, *Parankis*,
Feringhees, *Mundukaar*, and so on, especially in Kochi,
who accompanied and served the Portuguese and the
Dutch, were legally under them, worked in trades and

as labourers, and set up local families. What is distinctive about this group is that unlike other communities that claim purity of descent – or at least undergird their 'essence' through specific practices of marriage and inheritance – this is an eminently miscegenated one. Indeed, the Parankis bear traces of more than two cultures: among them there are traces of not only Portuguese culture and the non-Sanskritized and lower-caste cultures prevalent in Kerala, but also elements from South-east Asia, especially Java and Malacca, which were prominent centres of Dutch and Portuguese trade in the sixteenth and seventeenth centuries. But, unlike powerful merchant communities in Cochin, these miscegenated groups had neither the economic resources nor the political clout to integrate themselves into the caste hierarchy on terms advantageous to them. And unlike the Eurasians, their claims for inclusion in the groups that claimed 'purer' European blood were poor. And so the *Census of India* (1931), for instance, noted that though they did have a distinctly traceable foreign origin, the 'great majority of "firangis" [more commonly called Parankis – literally "Portuguese" in Malayalam] have at present, next to no admixture of foreign blood. They differ very little from Indian Christians'. From the 1931 Census Report, their predicament is clear: they may figure as 'Indian Christian', 'Firangis', and even as

'Anglo Indian' – or as none of these. And perhaps for this reason, it appears that they declined in numbers. Writing in the early twentieth century, the eminent historian K.P. Padmanabha Menon remarks that there were about 2539 Parankis in Kochi (1996: 441). In other words, the Parankis were already a minority within a minority even by the early twentieth century. The Cochin-Creole Portuguese language has no living speakers now, though once it was so vital that it thrived even under the successors of the Portuguese, the Dutch. Given this dismal history of decline within 'casteist-cosmopolitan' society, it is not surprising that prevailing academic and popular common sense about this group tends to reek of the stigma against miscegenation.

Thus the obsession with a fabulous past makes us blind to our lost histories. We tend to ignore the evidence in the historical record that the Parankis represent a more complex mix of people. For instance, there is historical evidence that the Portuguese brought a considerable number of Javanese from Malacca to Cochin – as early as Afonso de Albuquerque's return journey after the conquest of Malacca in 1511. These people were 'State' slaves – owned by the Sultan of Malacca who were not Muslim nor even converted Christians. Reis Thomaz notes that most of the slaves in Malacca were from Java, Sumatra, and the other islands. But these were *skilled* slaves, brought to teach local slaves trades useful to the Portuguese: Thomaz remarks that at the time of the Portuguese conquest in the early sixteenth century, slaves in Malacca earned almost the same wages as skilled free people (2000: 1820). The Javanese slaves were carpenters, boat-builders, mechanics, blacksmiths, sawyers, caulkers, gunners, makers of weapons and powder-magazines, who travelled with their families and often converted so that they would be free. But the Portuguese records also reveal that they were always not willing to be exported by their masters. There is evidence of slave mutinies aboard their ships and attempts to sail back to Java. Besides these people, Javanese and other South-east Asian people came to Cochin as crewmen in ships. It appears that almost all the crew of the ships that sailed from Malacca to Cochin throughout the 150 years of Portuguese presence – both those owned by the Portuguese Crown and the merchants – were manned by crew of South-east Asian origin. A third stream was opened through war. Later records indicate the presence of soldiers from South-east Asia in the forces of the Portuguese and the Dutch in the local wars in Cochin and Calicut. For instance, the Dutch campaign of 1663 involved ships manned by not just European but also Bandanese and Ambonese soldiers, a Ceylonese garrison, and the 'Mardijkers', an Indonesian-Dutch term that meant 'free people' or 'city people', referring to converted prisoners of war of mostly Asian background, and Batavian slaves. Indeed, there is a complete exciting transnational history to be recovered here, for there is evidence that slaves were very often taken to Batavia from the Malabar Coast, many of those who spoke Portuguese. Jean Gelman Taylor, who studied the social life of Batavia in the early seventeenth century, tells us that Portuguese became a popular language in Batavia through them. The celebrated historian of medieval Kerala, K.M. Panikkar mentions in passing that the desecration of the temple of the feudal nobleman Punnathur Nambidi by the Dutch forces in their campaign against Calicut in the eighteenth century was committed not by Europeans but by the Balinese soldiers under Dutch commanders. There are local traditions that speak of African slaves brought by the Portuguese to Cochin too. In short, the people known as 'Parankis' now represent a far more complex mix than that permitted by a vision of European conquest as essentially involving a neat and unambiguous division between an internally homogenous Western invader and an equally singular oppressed local society. Given that community assertion in a caste-ridden society is possible only within the framework of the caste hierarchy, and because caste society stigmatizes miscegenation, the

Parankis have been able to claim neither their complex past nor space within the history of Malayalee society. They have indeed figured in recent literary efforts to reclaim the multicultural legacy of Kochi, prominently in N.S. Madhavan's *Litanies of Dutch Battery* (2010), but as one of the elements that help in constructing its exotic allure. The 'subaltern cosmopolitanism' of the Parankis, increasingly lost in the flow of time, remains as obscured as ever in such attempts.

In contrast, Johny Miranda's *Jeevichirikkunnavarkku Vendiyulla Oppees: Requiem for the Living* meditates poignantly on the largely untold present of this small community. Clues about their 'subaltern cosmopolitanism' are strewn in this text. For example, in terms of address like *Nona* (in Indonesian-Dutch, refers to a locally born Creole woman, believed to come from the Portuguese 'Senhora' for 'lady' or 'madam') and *Choochi*, apparently a version of *Zusje* (Indonesian-Dutch for 'sister'). Or in descriptions of dress – *kavaya* and *thuni*, mentioned as the clothing distinctive of Paranki women indeed resembles the 'kebaya and sarong' worn all over South-east Asia by women. More importantly, Miranda's female characters, especially the formidable grandmother in the novella, have a remarkable resemblance with female Creole characters portrayed in the novels of Creole authors, especially the

Macanese de novelist Henrique de Senna Fernandes
and the Singaporean Rex Shelley. Running through the
novella is the narrator's awareness that the reader is most
likely to have no knowledge of the Parankis; therefore,
the narrative is broken more than once in the effort to
provide an 'anthropological introduction' to the reader.

Crisis and Hope

Requiem for the Living does not seek to be a substitute
for anthropological description. Nor is it a simplistic
attempt to claim and assert a community identity – and
indeed, this is what marks it as a unique literary effort. It
faces upfront the reality of the impossibility of asserting
miscegenated identities in a culture so obsessed with
purity of birth. Instead, it picks precisely this crisis as
its focus, and struggles to give expression to it through
the protagonist, the young Josy/Osha Periera (Osha
being the Creolized pronunciation of the Portuguese
name Jose). This may appear to be in sharp contrast to
the novels of community assertion, a long tradition in
modern Malayalam literature, stretching from the late
nineteenth century *Indulekha* and *Kundalata* to the
very recent *Kocharethi* (1998) (translated by Catherine
Thankamma as 'The Araya Woman') by Narayan. In
such novels, the consolidation of community identity

is achieved through narrating the life-journey of a female protagonist, whose trials and tribulations stand in place of the community struggling for self-definition and social space. Nevertheless, in many of these works, hidden behind the female figure, often, is the hand of the male reformer who shapes her subjectivity and directs her conduct in desirable ways. In *Requiem for the Living*, however, the central protagonist is definitely male – and he is precisely the reverse of the male reformer, marked by isolation, lack of voice, and powerlessness. Through him unfolds an extraordinary, intriguing tale of the community's slow merging into the bosom of the Roman Catholic Church, a dirge at its impending disappearance. And, indeed, there are female figures whose fate tells us much about the male protagonist's anxiety about the community, but we see them through Osha's helpless gaze.

The central axis of the crisis as seen by this young man is undoubtedly the deep divide between male and female authority figures. The present of the community seems marked by the pathos of fatherlessness. The father-figures in the novella are ineffectual, violent, or absent – it are the mothers who are the keepers of the community, carrying and handing down its hybrid customs, practices, and knowledges, and thus. The protagonist's grandmother – Juana Mammanji (possibly the Cochin-Creole version of *Mamae*) – is thus the centre around whom not only her family but also the whole community revolves: it is she who secured the economic stability of her family, kept the traditions and rituals of the local faith, which appear to be a hybrid of Catholic practices and local Hindu oracle-worship. Her husband was a weak man; her son, Osha's father, is a rebel whose revolt is pointless, feeble, and degrading; Osha is the very embodiment of the disempowered male. Osha's father's rebellion against the Catholic Church is silent and mostly self-destructive, but constant: in anger, he whispers abuse on Christ – *Jooda kazhuvery*. Jooda refers to Jesus' Jewish birth – and thus turns (Christian) anti-Semitism against Jesus himself. But in referring to him as a criminal condemned to death, it appears that the very hatred of the Jews of Christ's time against him is hurled back now. The anger here is not clearly classifiable – and it tells of the peculiar marginality that the Paranki male experienced. The unfolding of the crisis is narrated through two equally powerful strands of the narrative which follow Osha's search for identity and the fate of the women of his family, respectively, which meet at a crucial turn to reach an anguished climax.

This first strand begins with a major event early on in the narrative – at the age of twelve, Osha stumbles upon a small key in the soil thrown up when a grave was dug for the body of a pregnant woman in the cemetery. This discovery sets him on a search for its lock – and this becomes his obsession, the very quest of his life. This masterful (possibly phallic) metaphor indicates in no uncertain terms that the novella is about an identity – for identities, especially community identities, are like keys for which locks have to be found. It overshadows his life entirely – and therefore he can only watch the terrible tragedies which befall his mother and his sister. He even tries it on the lock of his grandmother's wooden box where she stored her ritual items, writing, and special clothes, but it does not fit. Osha is also searching for a special prayer which the male elders in his family alone recited, but without success. He however begins to drift away even as he searches, marrying Jacintha who is not a Paranki. But this does not soothe him; his agonized quest continues even on his wedding night and he is reluctant to consummate his marriage. However, eventually, Jacintha takes the initiative and they consummate their union, but he is plagued by nightmares. In this recurrent dream, Osha's sexual anxieties commingle with his anxieties about moving away from the community: he sees in this dream a pig-man buried for slaughter whose entrails explode as it suffocates to death underground. Jacintha is not unfamiliar with the mad quests of menfolk. Her own father is away at the pilgrimage centre of Velankkanni, seeking solace there. Right from the early days of their marriage, Jacintha disliked the key and wanted Osha to give it up, and finally she persuades him to give her his key. But when he gets to know of her pregnancy, he leaves Jacintha's house.

The second thread narrates the terrible fate of women in Osha's family. It too starts with the digging of the grave to bury the pregnant woman who died – which he witnesses at the age of twelve. Pregnant women, Osha says, represent unfulfilled wishes; they may wander as lost female souls, *yakshi*s. Perhaps they represent unrealized promises as well. The key emerges precisely from the depths in which such failed hopes must be buried. That Osha's grandmother, the pillar of their community, died about the same time he found the key, may not be coincidental. It marks the beginning of a period of total breakdown for the women in his family, who are seduced and betrayed. His mother, who had walked out of the joint family household in defiance of his grandmother, now begins to go astray. His sister, Ida, is betrayed in love first and returns home, quite possibly like a lost female soul rising up from the grave, as a yakshi. Indeed, seeing her back home, Osha feels that she 'now looked like a shattered tomb'. But caught up in his obsessive search, he watches ostensibly through the corner of his eye, her descent into madness and depravity, only to be hacked to death by their father. Indeed, Ida's fate is to suffer the death of hope, wander in madness and despair like a lost female soul, and then die pregnant, to be buried again with her Achilles' tendon cut so that she would not rise up again. Perhaps Ida was to be the object of reform, but she was not saved; Osha, who could be the reformer of the community (since in the whole text, it is he alone who might have achieved the necessary distance from the community), remains utterly passive.

However Ida's death – or her murder at the hands of the patriarch – changes her mother who returns and undergoes a total transformation, slipping into the matriarch's role with extraordinary smoothness. She inherits Mammanji's legacy and takes up her role in the community as the oracle, soothsayer, and custodian of its knowledge and practices. Interestingly enough, Osha and Ida's mother seems to possess the uncanny ability to smoothly re-enter the community and pick up its reins, leaving behind her earlier self completely. And this is, indeed, in sharp contrast with Osha's experience of both leaving the community through marriage (which, ironically, he could never really enter despite being born in it) and re-entering it. For Osha seeks solely the lock which his key can open, but he cannot find it.

The two strands come together to climax when Mamma takes over Mammanji's duties and powers.

Osha's anguish about intercourse – his unconscious fears about moving away from the community – becomes unbearable. He seeks the key again, only to find out that Jacintha and her mother had noticed that it was of gold and so they had sold it for money! Obviously, for Jacintha and her mother who are not Parankis, the key can have only material significance; they do not share the meanings that Osha unconsciously attaches to it. This flings him into a deep sense of loss, but even as he broods over it, he is overtaken by a series of momentous events – the death of his father and the discovery of Mammanji's sainthood during his burial. This anguish reaches a crescendo when the novella ends, when the protagonist's search ends in futility, and the community seems to be submerged by and merging with the Catholic Church. Yet this is not a total tragedy – for it also appears that the merging of the community in the larger Church may not be the end. Mammanji, the Oracle, the Soothsayer, is to become a Catholic saint, canonized by the Vatican! And this is achieved not through social reform and the enlightened male reformer, nor through the discovery of its 'truth' – or of the lock which the key may fit – but through its powerful women and the community's knowledge, rituals, and practices that they preserve.

It is hard to imagine a more honest dissection of the miscegenated community's crisis. True, this is indeed a man's story – but it is also a confession that the angst over a community's 'true essence' is primarily a masculine one. In this sense, *Requiem for the Living* richly deserves a unique place in this history of the novels of community-assertion in modern Malayalam literature. And for this reason, this extraordinary work of literature promises to be a critical event in contemporary Malayalam. I deliberately evoke the future tense here – for the work, though published for a while in Malayalam, was not yet discovered fully even in Kerala at the time it was chosen for translation into English. It is indeed an interesting event, too, in the history of translation from Indian languages into English, when a truly remarkable work of writing, mostly undiscovered in the former, is elevated to the attention it deserves through a translation. And in the light of our transnational histories that have been sacrificed so that 'high-Hindu-centric cosmopolitanism' may define modern Kerala, this, perhaps, is only poetic justice!

J. DEVIKA

Further Reading

Cardoso, Hugo. 2010. Interview by K. Pradeep, 'Tribute to Cochin Creole Portuguese', *The Hindu* Kochi Edition, 26 September.

Census of India. 1931. *Vol. 21 – Cochin*. Cochin: Government Press.

John, K.J. 1981. 'Emergence of Latin Christians in Kerala: A Brief Introduction', in *Christian Heritage of Kerala*, K.J. John (ed.). Kochi: L.M. Pylee Felicitation Committee, pp. 347–54.

Madhavan, N.S. 2010. *Litanies of Dutch Battery* (translated by Rajesh Rajamohan). New Delhi: Penguin.

Menon, K.P. Padmanabha. 1996. *History of Kerala*, vol. II. Chennai: AES.

Mostert, Tristan. 2007. 'Chain of Command: The Military System of the Dutch East India Company 1655–66'. MA Thesis submitted to the Department of History, University of Leiden.

Narayan. 1998. *Kocharethi* (translated as *The Araya Woman*, by Catherine Thankamma. New Delhi: OUP, 2011). Kottayam: D.C. Books.

Panikkar, K.M. 1931. *Malabar and the Dutch*. Bombay: D.B. Taraporevala and Sons.

Taylor, Jean Geldman. 2009. *The Social World of Batavia: Europeans and Eurasians in Colonial Indonesia*. Madison: University of Wisconsin Press.

Thomaz, Luis Filipe F. Reis. 2000. *Early Portuguese Malacca*. Macau: Macau Territorial Commission for the Commemorations of the Portuguese Discoveries.

'It seems to me rather useless to spend time in reading what is unintelligible and can therefore bear no fruit. I never could understand the fondness some people have for confusing their minds by dwelling on mystical books that merely awaken their doubts and excite their imagination, giving them a bent for exaggeration quite contrary to Christian simplicity. Let us rather read the Epistles and Gospels. Let us not seek to penetrate what mysteries they contain; for how can we, miserable sinners that we are, know the terrible and holy secrets of Providence while we remain in this flesh which forms an impenetrable veil between us and the Eternal? Let us rather confine ourselves to studying those sublime rules which our divine Saviour has left for our guidance here below. Let us try to conform to them and follow them, and let us be persuaded that the less we let our feeble human minds roam, the better we shall please God, who rejects all knowledge that does not come from Him; and the less we seek to fathom what He has been pleased to conceal from us, the sooner will He vouchsafe its revelation to us through His divine Spirit.'

—PRINCESS MARY,
in her letter to Julie Karagina
in Leo Tolstoy's *War and Peace*

Juana Mammanji

My name is Josy Pereira. They call me Osha. My Pappa's name is Franso Pereira. Mamma's, Petrina Pereira. Pappanji's name is Caspar, but they call him Caipar. Mammanji's name is Juana, but Joona is what they call her.

Pappa has four younger brothers: Alsocha, Visenthiyacha, Sandhyavacha, and Johnacha. And for all of them, a sister, Rosy, whom they call Kosamma.

Years ago, Pappanji's Pappa had arrived at this village of ours, Ponjikkara, on a country boat. In those early days, they had settled on a piece of land that belonged to a seth in Mattancherry and lay abandoned and overrun with creepers and bushes. They cleared it, fenced off a compound, and built a house with bamboo, palm leaves, and strips of areca wood.

It was Juana Mammanji who built the imposing *tharavad*, one sees today, with mortar and laterite stone; a house that could be considered grand for those days. A house with facing windows and doors large enough for souls to come and go easily; with a verandah, a large hall, and an attic.

Pappanji's Pappa's name too was Franso. From Pappanji's time, the sacristans of the church have all been members of our family. One by one, his six elder brothers left for Chavara with their families, and Pappanji alone stayed back here with his sacristan work and small shop.

It was Pappa who took over as sacristan from Pappanji. He also got the shop, which stocked every possible thing from salt to soda.

Though we were Parankis, the men in our family weren't the kind who wore trousers. Instead, they wore the *mundu* and the half-sleeved shirt called *kammeesa*. The earlier generations used to wear broad waistbands as well, into which they would tuck betel leaves, tobacco, and lime to make their chewing mixture.

As for the women, called *choochi*s, they wore the traditional clothing of *thuni* and *kavaya*.

These thunis, similar to mundus, were printed with large blue or red checks. The collar-less kavayas, stitched from fabric of bright colours and shiny patterns, were held together with copper pin-hooks and worn with their long sleeves rolled-up.

They also wore beaded gold chains called kotheenjas.

In her left hand, Juana Mammanji always carried a small cloth bag with money in it.

Everyone wore the scapular called *ventheenja*; you rarely saw them without it. They were bought by the lot and blessed at the Arthungal Church where people would go with their families for the yearly festival.

Wearing that ventheenja, Mammanji would say, made it easy for women to give birth; and it protected everyone from ghosts, spirits, demons, and fear.

It was a custom for the whole family to go together for the Arthungal Church festival every year.

After crossing the river by country boat, we then walked along the beach. Setting out in the evening, people walked all night, chattering, singing, praying, eating, drinking, laughing, and playing along the way, reaching Arthungal as dawn broke in the east. The day was spent there.

The people who lived near the church would have vacated their homes and gone elsewhere. Their pots and pans and stoves would be waiting for the pilgrims in those houses. The pilgrims could use them as their own; so long as they left them exactly as they had found them.

Once – it was said – at the time of the festival, the locals had refused to leave their homes for the pilgrims! That year, the Saint of Arthungal unleashed a terrible pox on the locals. They became frantic.

One night, the Saint appeared in a dream to the vicar: this is punishment for the mischief they did to my children. The vicar announced the news to the parish. Not once since then have the parishioners failed to vacate their homes for the pilgrims.

By the time they returned from Arthungal, their purses would be empty, having spent all on household goods, coloured candy, sugarcane, fries, puffed rice, date fruit, glass bangles, toys, and much else besides....

Everything would be tied in a bundle and hung from a wooden pestle, which would then be carried by two people on their shoulders.

Before leaving, the younger men would visit the Arthungal beauties who would be waiting for them on the beach; the real purpose of their pilgrimage, after all. When they got back, friends who hadn't gone for the pilgrimage would ask, 'Dirtied your dongs, did you?'

Our Pappanji Casparacha had preserved the purity and integrity of sacristan work. The curse of God that most men earn with that job never fell on Pappanji.

Pappanji was a milksop. In Mammanji's words, 'a good-for-nothing ...'!

It was thanks to Mammanji's skills that they managed to get by. Besides running the provision store, she would make breakfast snacks – *appam, puzhungunda, chukkunda, puttu, idiyappam* – put them into containers and hand them to the children to sell all over the village.

Made from white rice that was bought, washed, soaked, pounded in the mortar, and steamed by Mammanji herself, these dishes were famed for their taste.

A rumour had spread among the villagers that Mammanji had got up and pounded rice immediately after giving birth to her youngest, Kosamma aunty. And therefore, those snacks smelt of blood.

The blood-smell of toil.

Everyone in the village respected and even feared Juana Mammanji. She even had a nickname: 'Judge Nona'.

Not just in the family, but in the whole parish, everything concerning what was to be done when a child was born or when someone died, or simply about things to be followed in everyday life ... in all such matters, it was to Mammanji that they turned for advice.

That pregnant women should not be godmothers at a baptism, that you should give a pregnant woman anything she asked for, the rules concerning pollution that related to new mothers, that brothers and sisters should not get married at the same time at the same venue; it seems such beliefs had spread in the village from Mammanji!

Mammanji even wrote a booklet about the conventions to be followed in making holy bread and sauce during the Pesaha season, and distributed it in church before Holy Week.

The gist of its contents read thus:

The faithful should see the Pesaha bread and sauce as symbols of the flesh and blood of the crucified Christ.

Therefore, those who prepared the bread and sauce had to observe esthi; *had to bathe, purify themselves and fast before they began.*

No one was to pick at, nibble, or taste the ingredients when they were being prepared. Even the water from the coconuts broken for it was not to be used for anything else.

Those used to munching bits when coconuts were grated, had to try and overcome that temptation.

No flavouring was to be added to the traditional ingredients for unleavened bread – flour, black gram, a bit of garlic, and some salt. Apart from coconut milk, jaggery syrup, flour, and some cardamom, nothing was to be added to the sauce, for the sake of indulgence.

None of these items were to be prepared in vessels used for cooking meat or fish.

*The palm fronds blessed and handed out at church
on Palm Sunday were to be preserved on the stand which
held the fuskya icons. Finger-length strips were to be torn
from them and laid across each other to form a cross on
the dough in the vessels. Thereafter, the breads had to be
steam-cooked.*

*Once cooked, the breads were to be laid on a white
cloth spread on a table set before the holy icons. Only then
should the household leave for mass on Maundy Thursday,
followed by the Washing of the Feet ceremony and the
Adoration of the Cross.*

*Upon returning, the head of the household breaks the
bread in the presence of all the family members. He then dips
pieces of the bread in the sauce and distributes it to everyone.*

At the tharavad, everyone thought it a revolutionary
act for Mammanji to break Pesaha bread and distribute
it, even though Pappanji was officially the head of the
household. She would also take the initiative to get
people to practice reciting the *Puthenpaana* in their
homes on Good Friday.

During the days of Lent, there is a ritual of calling
Devastha in the coastal regions. Held after midnight,
usually only men would take part in it, holding wooden
crosses and wooden bells. In this ceremony too, it was
Mammanji who took the lead.

If a child fell sick, people would run to Juana Mammanji. She had a famous cure for inflamed tonsils. Garlic and the bud of the coral flower were mashed together to make an ointment. Chewed tobacco and betel leaf was then spat on it. This mixture was first applied on the child's forehead, and then rubbed hard on the throat. A three-day treatment and the child would recover completely ...!

Mammanji's other remedy was to heat the handle of a wooden ladle and press it against the throat, over the inflamed tonsils.

For mumps, the prescriptions included hanging a coconut shell around the neck and beatings with the courtyard broom. Or else, Mammanji would make a paste by mixing the ashes of a soiled menstrual cloth with oil, and use a feather to rub it all over the patients face ...!

As for jaundice, no matter how far gone or severe, three days of treatment was all it took her to cure it ...!

Mammanji's medicine was in a capsule form, made from a paste of the tender leaves of the castor plant, ground with fennel seeds. Usually, patients were not allowed salted food or oil on their scalp before a bath. But for those who took Mammanji's cure, nutritious food with salt was a must, as was an oil bath twice a day.

Mammanji would forbid only a few items in their diet, like chicken, eggs, and tamarind. Even allopathic doctors were cured of bad cases of jaundice by Mammanji's prescription.

Mammanji would bathe several times a day, but not once would she dry her long hair. Instead, she'd tie it up, still wet, in a bundle. Nor did she ever fall ill from doing this.

The first Fridays of every month were special days for Mammanji. That day she would wear a glittering new silk kavaya with shiny flowers on it. She would then put on her kotheenja, a silver bangle, a string with a gold cross on it, a scapular tied with holy remains, the shoes called sappath, and finally fix a large hat on her head. All these were specially readied for that day.

On that morning, Juana Mammanji would first go to church where there would be special services. She would attend every one of them.

That day, the family shop would be closed. Not just her sons and daughter, but the kunjathas and kunjathos, kumbaris and kumbarichis, peelas children and nonas and susis, would have all assembled at home with much purity and piety, having set aside their own chores.

In the tharavad hall, in vasis arranged on a large table covered with white linen, dishes like puttu, lathiri, or noolappam and mullet curried in coconut milk, along with cheroots and bowls of toddy would be placed. After church, Mammanji would head straight to the riverside. There too, people would be waiting with the utmost devotion.

Mammanji would enter the water wearing all her ornaments, immerse herself completely, and leave the river, dripping wet. Her return trip to the house and the crowd gathered there was a sight worth seeing....

Clicking her fingers in a peculiar rhythm, dancing to the tune of a strange song which no one had heard before, sung in a melody no one could imitate, in words no one understood, she would walk home from the riverside.

On her way, she would stare at each and every one, checking if everyone was wearing their ventheenjas. If anyone was caught without one, Mammanji would spit on their faces with a loud cackle!

Then she would make detailed predictions about everyone's future. Make proclamations in answer to the queries of the anxious. Prescribe offerings. She would scold those who were lazy about attending prayer and church, those who slept at those times without observing esthi.

Then, humming that same tune, she would lie belly down on the dishes set on the table. Mammanji would not taste even one of them....

After a while, she'd get up and lie on her back, on the full-length plantain leaf that would have been cut and laid out in advance. She would then slip into a deep sleep, as if she had lost consciousness.

By then, the food and drink on the table would have been completely drained of their taste and aroma, and turned into mere refuse. No one ever touched them. They were simply thrown into the river. Even the fish did not touch them, it was said.

There was also talk that in that state, Mammanji could even levitate, and could lie atop the large leaf of one of the plantain trees that stood by the courtyard! On some rare days, Mammanji had demonstrated it too. Not only would the leaf not break from her weight, it would not even shake or sway as much as it would have, had a crow sat on it.

Once Mammanji regained her posture – it was said – the leaf, along with the whole tree, would collapse with a loud thump!

How brightly Mammanji's face would glow at those times, as if she had been transformed into someone else! When she woke, Mammanji would say she recalled nothing of what had happened.

Mammanji, and everyone else, believed that it was from this ritual that she got the strength for everything after Caspar Pappanji's death. Or even before that.

In her old age, Mammanji withdrew from her responsibilities, shut herself in her room, and not uttering a word to anyone, sat reading the Holy Bible in the light of the hurricane lamp.

She would get up only when her hair got dry. Then, opening the door, she would go to the well and haul up bucketsful of water and pour it on her head. She would then tie up her wet hair and return to the room. Whenever she wasn't reading the Bible, you could see her filling sheet after sheet of very white paper with tiny scribbles.

She ate only once a day, and not much either ...

And so it was that one day, when she did little else but read and write, Juana Mammanji died, with her eyes open and gazing into the Holy Book.

From the Grave, a Gold Chaavi

I don't know how my Pappa came to hate sacristan work and the Paranki race so much.

So what if we call ourselves Parankis and have these surnames, none of us knows English, nor have trousers or coats or shoes.

Dark skin, rough, shrunken cheeks, bloated eyelids, centipede moustache, baldness, rotten teeth, pot belly, and dwarfish build; these are the common features of the men in our family.

When the coastal people – the lowest of low in wealth, education, caste, and living standards – were converted, all that they were really given were some

four hundred surnames. Yours too are among those; this
venom was injected into us by none other than some
suited-booted English-speaking Parankis.

Paranki scum, with only surnames to show for
themselves!

Perhaps, Pappa had realized this. When there was
no one in the church, Pappa would turn to the rathaal,
and pointing at the crucifix, call out loudly ... 'Jooda
Kazhuvery! Jooda Kazhuvery!'

It was his duty to ring the church bell that hung from
the tamarind tree, three times a day, without fail. But
Pappa never bothered. At those times, he'd be staggering
about, drunk on arrack mixed with watermelon juice.

Pappa would receive the Holy Communion after
having sex; without fasting, without bathing, without
observing esthi. He would wipe the reliquary clean and
place it on the altar, place the sanku and casa on the
sacristy. On the altar thochas, he would light the candles
for Holy Mass. Put flowers in the venthosas, burn incense,
spread out the vestments of appropriate colour for the
day, mark the portions to be read in the prayer books.

I have seen Pappa stealing and drinking communion
wine, and adding water to the rest. Pappa would blow out
candles lit by the faithful in the church and the cemetery
as soon as they had left. He would later melt them and sell
them at the price of wax and get drunk on that money.

If anyone died in the parish, it was Pappa's duty as sacristan to show the gravedigger where to dig the grave in the cemetery. Only Pappa knew who had been under the earth long enough for their graves to be dug again. When they removed the old wooden crosses from those graves, Pappa would take them and nail them to the board walls of our house. (Our family of four – Pappa, Mamma, me, and Chitta – had moved out of the tharavad.)

Colluding with the church wardens, he would steal coconuts, palm-stalks, and things from the church property and bring them home. When the offering-box was opened, he would secretly slip the larger notes into his pocket....

Pappa also pilfered coins dropped in the bowls by the faithful for reciting Anatha.

When someone died, looking forward to the money it would bring him and the church, Pappa would say to himself: 'Oh, it's a lucky day ... I'm saved for today ...'.

Pappa had once lived in joy and peace and plenty with his brothers and sister and Pappanji and Mammanji in the tharavad. After all, it was on seeing that house and its glory and its life that Mamma's parents from the neighbouring village had got her married to Pappa, with lots of money and gold as dowry.

In a year's time though, Mamma had had enough of life at the tharavad. Joona Mammanji's dictatorial and rigid ways, her rules and decrees, had not agreed with Mamma at all.

Mamma defied Mammanji, whom no one had dared to oppose. She broke the rules. That was how Mammanji came to disapprove of Pappa and Mamma.

Pappa bought this shack by selling Mamma's gold. He ended up following Mamma out of the tharavad. Had Mamma called him to Hell itself, Pappa would have gone along. Mamma was that beautiful.

Since the income from sacristan work was not enough for him, Pappa would go rope-fishing with the fisher folk. Or with the Muslims to haul stone and sand as a wage-labourer, or to pull handcarts.

Mamma did not allow Pappa to name me for Pappanji, nor my Chitta Ida for Mammanji.

Idamma Chitta was born the same year they got married. I was born three years later. My birth was in the newly bought shack. Idamma's, in the tharavad.

When Ida Chitta was born, Mammanji's stern rules and exacting after-birth care caused Mamma much emotional distress and physical torment.

Juana Mammanji must have plucked the leaves of the pepper plant that would have had crept up the areca tree in the yard, and placing the dried rind of the gambooge fruit on it, heated both, and pressed the hot pack into Mamma's genitals, tying it tightly with a cloth.

It was one of Mammanji's treatments for new mothers and was meant to help remove the wastes from the womb ...! A treatment that caused much burning and pain.

For fifteen days after childbirth, no curry with her rice for the new mother; only a chutney ground with chilli. As for drink, all that she would be allowed with a meal was a tumbler of water! She had to make do with that to rinse her mouth and satisfy her thirst.... This, at a time when women were said to be so thirsty they could drink a whole well dry.

Mammanji would also serve as midwife. As soon as the baby came out, there was a notorious 'belly-press' that Mammanji would perform with both hands on the mother's abdomen. More painful than the birth itself, I have heard it said. What was an attempt to remove the placenta, Mamma might have misunderstood as an act of vengeance.

Mammanji would insist that a knife and a broom be placed at all times at the head of the new mother's bed. It was to protect the child from the evil eye. If a child had not teethed, Mammanji would not allow it to be taken outdoors in its swaddling clothes after six in the evening.

To rid the child and its mother of the evil eye, first, some dried chilli and salt was wrapped in paper and waved silently over them. Then the wrapping was spat on and the packet thrown in the stove; the 'eye' would then lose its effect!

If the packet thrown in the fire did not explode, and if those who caught the fumes from it did not cough, it confirmed that the 'eye' had fallen on either the child or the mother ...!

Our house, made of wooden boards nailed in rows and painted black, had almost no courtyard. For that reason, we did not have our own toilet either. Pappa and I used the grounds near the church-landing. Or we crouched in the dense taro bush behind the cemetery ...

My Mamma and Ida Chitta did their toilet and had their baths indoors. A corner of the house had been screened off with old clothes, behind which they would do it in an old cooking bowl and keep it covered. At night, Pappa would take it and dump it in the river.

Only once a week would Mamma take a proper bath, washing her hair, pouring water over her head. It would be at the public tap, late at night when the street was completely empty, with Pappa standing guard.

In those days, whenever it rained, Mamma and Ida Chitta would go and stand outside so that it did not go waste. For Mamma, a bath usually meant rubbing herself with a wet cloth wrung out....

How irresponsibly he had lived, my Pappa!

It was only after I had grown up that a separate bathroom, a lean-to, was made with thatch in the corner of that tiny compound, and a small well dug. All these, the consequences of leaving the tharavad.

Let me mention an incident from a time before my memory. It was the night of the vespera of St. Sebastian's kombreria festival at the parish church. Pappa and Ida Chitta were in the church. As I was small and had yet to teeth, Mamma had stayed back with me.

I lay alone in a room. Mamma was in the kitchen, and I was crying loudly. Had we been in the tharavad under Mammanji's care, I would never have lain alone at night. As I lay crying, an owl flew in and sat on me, fluttering its wings all over me. It was cuddling me out of love. Mammanji used to say that owls liked babies that hadn't teethed. It seems that that was how I caught bird-fever in childhood, and my limbs had shrivelled.

Pappa had stopped my studies in the lower class itself and passed on the sacristan's duties to me.

It happened when I was nearly twelve years old. Someone – a pregnant woman – had died.

There is a belief that when pregnant women die, they turn into yakshis. After all, death has come to them before their earthly wishes have been fulfilled. It is said that they collect seeds of pavonia and tamarind, and bits of glass bangles and flowers. That they crave to caress babies and wander around in deserted places, singing to themselves.

Once upon a time, a child went missing. In those days, bushes and creepers grew wild all around. The villagers searched everywhere possible. Looked in the ponds and canals. Combed the bushes and the undergrowth. Finally, when they went searching deep within the woods, guess what they came upon ...?

A beautiful yakshi under a large banyan tree, swinging the child in a cradle of kolamariya flower vines and singing melodiously....

When the villagers approached pointing a long cross at her, the yakshi spat at them and fled into the woods, leaving the child swinging in the cradle.

But what if they got the baby back, it had lost its sight ...!

That child had to make a living as a street singer, wandering all over town and country. Its voice, a boon from the yakshi, was said to be incomparably sweet.

I had gone along with Pappa when he went to show the gravedigger where to bury the body of the pregnant woman. I stood there, watching the gravedigger at work.

Every time a grave is dug, there are always people who gather to watch and enjoy themselves. They would examine the remains in the old grave very closely. The sight of skulls, especially, was a gratifying experience for them....

Clods of sticky white earth, scooped up by the gravedigger with a hoe, kept falling as near as my feet. It caught my eye suddenly. A glint of gold between the clods. I bent down and picked it up. It was a gold chaavi, the size of a little finger. I didn't know it was gold. I did not bother to find out. I knew no one else had seen it. I put it in the pocket of my shorts.

I told no one about that key, carrying it with me like a treasure. Once, when no one was watching, I inserted it in the lock that hung from the chain that secured the house door. Later, on different occasions and for different reasons, I kept secretly trying it on the locks of houses, churches, and even the school. Whenever I went to a neighbouring village on some errand, I took that chaavi along with me. When I attended church festivals too, I took it along.

Those days, the very purpose of my travels had been reduced to a search for the lock of that chaavi....

The Curse of God Upon The Sacristan

'Mon ... I knew you'd come ... I had an inkling ... The raven was crowing its heart out to tell us....'

This was how Mamma would greet Xavy in those days. After all, it is only the arrival of one's dearest that the raven crows its heart out to tell.

'Idamma ... look ... Xavy is here ...' Mamma would say, before sending him off to Ida Chitta's room. It could hardly be called a room. An old saree draped in a corner, screening it off like a partition. There they were; Ida Chitta, all of eighteen years and as pretty as Mamma, and a youthful Xavy.

By then, Mamma would have set out for the teashop, a bottle in hand.

Xavy was from the neighbouring village. Must have been about twenty. A young and strapping stone-mason, he was a distant relation of Mamma's.

Xavy always had plenty of cash on him whenever he came. He would also bring clothes and things to eat.

'Xavy says he wants to marry her ...' Mamma would go around telling everyone.

While buying tea and snacks at the teashop, she would tell the shopkeeper, loud enough for everyone else to hear: 'Xavy has come. This is for him....'

That day, returning home from church after ringing the evening bell, I could tell there was someone with Ida Chitta behind the saree-wall. I peeked inside ... after all, it was my own house. And what did I see there ... Xavy and Ida Chitta....

I slipped out quietly without them knowing. Sometimes, Xavy would go back only in the morning. I would try not to get home until Xavy had left. Pappa did the same.

If Pappa came home and Xavy was around, Mamma would tell him sternly, 'You don't sleep here tonight. There's no room here ...'.

Pappa had got used to sleeping in the cemetery or on the veranda of the church or the school. As for me, I cannot sleep at all in any of those places, even if I try.

One day, Mamma sent Ida Chitta and Xavy off somewhere together on the boat. She returned and went from door to door, announcing to anyone who would listen: 'Xavy ran away with my daughter ...'

But, after two weeks, Ida Chitta came back. Alone. She wasn't the same Chitta who had left home. Chitta now looked like a shattered tomb.

Mamma's trick had not worked.

In her last days, Mammanji would say, over and over: 'Franso, you have the curse of God upon you, the curse of God ...'.

How many times had Mammanji spat squarely on Pappa's face as he stood with folded hands on the first Fridays of every month. How many times had he been scolded. Later, he had stopped visiting Mammanji altogether, fearing punishment.

'Many generations will pay for your sins as sacristan,' Mammanji would tell Pappa. He would only mutter to himself: 'Whose sins am *I* paying for then ...'.

No one could match Pappa in the sheer variety of cuss words he knew. Pappa would go anywhere without even wearing a shirt. Sometimes, he would walk around the house, stark naked. Or go to sleep that way. When Mamma was not around, he would eat up the rice in the pot down to the last bit, and then piss in it. Sometimes, he'd shit in the stove.

It was Pappa's habit to have tea at the teashop and then leave the coin in the glass.

Sometimes, on his way to take a shit by the church-landing at dawn, he would stop by the idol of St. Anthony in the cupola. He would fix a lit beedi in the saint's hand, and say: 'Smoke one, Anthony, smoke ... beedi smoke is good for this chill ...'.

With every day that passed, Pappa's antics got worse. During the parish festival one year, a drunk Pappa set fire to a string of crackers.

Now, the sacristan might help the chemmador, and the chemmador might help the sacristan. If the church choir is absent, the sacristan might even sing during the service. But, the sacristan never tries to help with the fireworks on festival day.

The crackers exploded unexpectedly and Pappa got burnt all over. Fearing for his life, Pappa jumped into the river. That was how Pappa lost an eye and four fingers, and got those white scars all over his body.

Now the parishioners too said: 'The curse of God has fallen on Fransocha ... the curse of God!'

On the Day of Judgement, when all shall rise from their graves in answer to the voice of God, they would all be hungry and thirsty. So that they do not lack for food, God shall bring forth a bounty even in the desert. On that day, God shall separate the maimed, and condemn them. God shall ask Pappa: 'Where is an eye of yours? Where are four of your fingers? Why is your skin not whole ...? Why did you not try to be buried in the fullness of the body I gave you? Hell awaits you, Franso. For you, Hell.'

It was with that incident that the vicar sacked Pappa from the sacristan's post. At the age of just eighteen, I was appointed sacristan.

The only reason Pappa was kept on until then – despite several forceful complaints from the parishioners – was that I had already been performing most of the sacristan's duties.

On waking in the morning, and before going to bed at night, every male in our family – from Pappanji onwards – would recite a prayer. It was written by

Pappanji's Pappa, Franso Pappanji, on a scrap of paper, in thick, stark lead. A copy had been given to the head of every household. Those outside our family would find it very difficult to read from those scraps. Perhaps even impossible.

It was said that those old, soiled, yellowed scraps of paper spread a peculiar fragrance. While everyone stored it safely like a holy relic, and handed it over to one of their sons like a family treasure, my Pappa alone lost it.

I had searched for that scrap of paper many times over, but never found it. To this day, I search for it. I look for it everywhere; in the rusted old iron trunks, in the rosewood chest fitted with bronze-work that Mamma brought as her dowry, in the Bible, in books like *Puthenpaana*, *Vanakkamaasam*, *Mar Alleshucharitham*, *Genoaparvam*, and *Istakicharitham*.... But I never found it.

It was around the time Ida Chitta ran away with Xavy that Petrina Mamma changed her attire from thuni and kavaya to saree and blouse.

When thirty-eight year old Mamma wore a saree, she looked a lot younger than her age. The blouse, with its wide, low-cut neck and the saree worn fetchingly below the navel, made Mamma's youthful beauty and charm glow even more.

Mamma took the thunis and kavayas out into the courtyard and burned them.

She had made Ida Chitta wear long-skirts and blouses as a child. And saree and blouse, after she had come of age.

It must have been a year after Chitta returned that Mamma left me and Chitta and Pappa and ran away with Chitta's lover Xavy. With Xavy, who was so many years younger than her ...!

A Church Bell that had Never been Rung

The very day Father Varghese took charge as the new vicar, he had me pull down two tender coconuts from the church tree. He then got me to buy two bottles of *kottodi*, and drank it mixed with water and coconut water before dinner.

Sometimes, the new vicar would drink up the communion wine, and I would have to add water, so it would not fall short. Every time there was a baptism, wedding or funeral, along with the contribution to the church, the flock started bringing a bottle of arrack too as a gift for their shepherd.

In former times, brides and grooms had to pass the marriage catechism before their engagement to get the 'marriage permission slip'. Now they could get it with a bottle. Such was the state of affairs in the parish.

The previous vicar, Father Raymond, had made it mandatory to pass the catechism. He had even increased the number of prayers to be recited, making the marriage slip a stumbling block for most.

The frustrated young people of the parish concluded that the vicar had done so out of spite, being unable to marry himself. That was how after mass one Sunday, forty young men and women gathered in protest at the oval stone steps at the church's entrance, and in view of the whole parish, raised their hands skywards and vowed, 'We shall not marry until Father Raymond leaves this parish'. Such was the tradition of this parish.

Had Father Varghese come here earlier, perhaps Pappa would not have been fired from the sacristan's post.

The parish is crisscrossed by canals, and everywhere there are empty lots run over by bushes. There are still some who are afraid to step out alone after dark. In the evenings, the whole place fills with the smell of Kappiri Muthappans boiling cassava.

But then, during Lent, does not the devout walk these roads even at midnight to call Devastha and to attend mass? For them, the Holy Church is still the one made of stone and mortar. They would like nothing better than to attend as many masses as possible before they died and enter them all in the ledger of life. Such people get the priests and sacristans they deserve.

Humiliated by Pappa, betrayed by Xavy, and abandoned by Mamma, one day Ida Chitta secretly took a boat to the crowded city nearby.

For a long time, she had wandered about the village, a madwoman. The parishioners used to feed and clothe her. Even so, she left our village.

She would sit by the edge of the roadside canal in which flowed shit and filth, swinging her legs in the water, tattling to passers-by about how scared she was to stay in the house even during the day. She would tell them that a demon inhabited the southern corner of the house. There he'd sit, sucking on a cigar and blowing smoke, his eyes bulging. Whenever he got a chance, he would grab her by the hair and hit her on her back, or try to pluck out her nipples.

Ida Chitta would not stop telling people that our house sat on an old cremation ground, that Pappa had no thoughts of marrying his daughter off though she had come of age, that he was keeping her there only to get her beaten by the demon, that when Mamma was around, the demon would try to grab her too whenever he got a chance, that it was Mamma who protected the demon....

I had come to know that Chitta was roaming the city streets day and night. What could I have done.... At that time, I too had been wandering aimlessly with my chaavi.

Chitta seemed to have liked the city, where she could dance wantonly and enjoy herself with lusty savages every night. And the larger the crowd, the louder she would laugh, it was said!

After Ida Chitta and Mamma left, Pappa brought a karambi to stay with him. I have heard Pappa boasting shamelessly about his virility. Why then, I still wonder, had Mamma run away?

But what I just said is a lie. The truth is that I rarely think about all that. Sitting by myself in the cemetery, or at the riverside when it is deserted, all I think about is that gold chaavi. Laying it on my open palm, I would sit there just looking at it....

Like the fat, shiny, white maggot that comes out when a grave is dug, it keeps crawling through my brain and my mind. Sometimes I think that I should just throw that chaavi into the river or into the pit where the skulls and bones from old graves are dumped. But I've not been able to. To this day, I have been searching for its lock.

In spite of my family's past, and even when they knew I did not earn enough to support a wife, I managed to get a proposal for marriage. The bride was Jacintha, daughter of Achamma Chechi, who lived in a vast compound with four cows and no man in the house.

To ensure protection for her daughter and herself, she had installed hallowed snake-deities in all four corners of the compound, at which she lit lamps every day. On the first Friday of every month, she made offerings and said prayers to the Saint of Edappally, and once a year, gave a rooster. They were Mappila Latin Christians, who wore thrice-washed white full-blouses and mundu, and finger-thick earrings in their upper ears.

They never lacked the cow dung required for the three washings. The clothes, kept immersed in cow dung water, were not washed with soap. Instead, ash from the wood-stove would be mixed with water and left in a basin for a day, and the next day she would drain the clear liquid on top and wash clothes in it.

Achamma Chechi fed the cows herself. She scooped up the dung, cleaned the shed, and milked the cows. Jacintha only delivered the milk from house to house. Apart from homes, she also brought milk to the church and the teashop. Though she was of marriageable age, she was not embarrassed to deliver milk. Perhaps, because she had been used to it from a young age.

Every morning, she came to the kuseenja with milk for the vicar. I saw her every day, but not once had I talked to her. But then, which girl had I ever talked to....

She had often spoken to me, or asked me about things, but only what was absolutely necessary.

There was just one thing that Achamma Chechi insisted on: after the wedding I had to move into their house and stay with Jacintha.

I let myself get married without even being aware of it, the way a cow allows itself to be milked.

Pappa, Mamma, Chitta, no one attended the wedding. But Pappa's family came out in force to organize the wedding. Mine was the first wedding in that generation of the family. Following everyone's wishes, the wedding celebrations were held at the tharavad. Before the groom's party set out, candles were lit and prayers said before the framed portraits of Pappanji and Mammanji.

The ceremonies were all according to Paranki custom. On many occasions, we felt Mammanji's absence. How beautifully Mammanji would sing the Laudatha, the prayer song of praise, after the first row of guests had finished their meals.

Everyone in the family agreed that the first night should be spent in the tharavad. In that room, on that same bed on which Juana Mammanji had lived out her last days.

A room that lay sunk in darkness even by day, filled with cold air, the odour of ages refusing to leave it, its walls faded, its ceiling lined with decaying wooden planks oozing a powdery rot…. Is it possible for a room to change so much over time?

At night, the sounds of scampering, squeaking mice filled the room. Mammanji's Bible and prayer books lay on the table, covered in dust. The thocha on which Mammanji used to light candles still stood on the wooden stand that held the fuskya icons. Facing it, stood Pappanji's and Mammanji's portraits.

'I feel scared in this room …', Jacintha said to me.

But, at that time, I was experiencing a serenity, security, and peace that I had not known until then. A feeling as if I had entered my own realm. If only I could live with Mammanji in this house, in this room!

I forgot about Jacintha. She was about to start some conversation. I didn't pay any attention. Sometime later, I said: 'Let's go to sleep'.

Sometime in the middle of the night, thinking she was asleep, I got up from the bed. When the old rope bed creaked and shuddered, my insides shuddered with it.

There she lay on the bed, like a beautiful, decorated idol that had been flung aside. Her breasts rose forth from between the unsettled saree folds. Her navel was like a great flower in bloom.

I untied the end of my mundu. Picked up the chaavi. The ever-burning lamp on the stand gave out enough light. I planted my eyes on Mammanji's rosewood chest fitted with ornamental bronze-work.

Outside, I thought I heard someone go by on a horse in full gallop, the hooves echoing. And with it, the sound of a whip or a sword being swirled in the air with great force.

Inserting the chaavi into the lock, I realized that it did not belong to this chest either. I found some sheets of paper on top of the chest. Sheets that were filled with scribbles from end to end. I read them all in that dim light in one sitting. Among other things, they contained recipes of nostrums for all kinds of ills, and practices to be followed on all occasions; at birth, in life, after death. Among these scribbles, what attracted me most were the writings about death and funeral rites.

Mammanji was born under the sign of Sagittarius, and because she was born in that particular hour of that month, it was said she could see that what was invisible to others: among them, spirits, and saints who rode on chariots ...!

I did not sleep a wink that night. Did not embrace or kiss Jacintha. Why, did not even look at her once with desire, or tenderness....

Later, I realized that I was mistaken to think Jacintha was asleep that night. What woman on her first night would fall asleep, and snore, in the company of a stranger....

She would have wished for so much....

Jacintha, like a church bell that had never been rung!

As usual, I got up at daybreak to ring the church bell. In the church yard, I saw all the usual sights: the clamour of dogs playing in the wet grass; at the oval stone steps, the congregation of frogs that had come to eat the wax....

That very day, Jacintha and I left for her house. My mother-in-law Achamma Chechi had arranged for a boy to deliver milk in Jacintha's place. The mixed odour of cow dung and milk always hung about Jacintha's house and surroundings. It stirred neither pleasure nor revulsion in me. The nose for me is just an instrument to breathe with.

The next night too, Jacintha came to bed all dressed up, wearing jasmine flowers in her hair. I did not touch her that night as well. We slept without sleeping. Woke without waking ...!

She must have made offerings to Our Lady of Velankanni and St. Anthony to change my mind. Must have wept and prayed a lot....

Another Seeker

It was on the third day after my wedding that I heard the news. I had just locked the church door and was on my way back home after a seventh-day memorial service and an oppees performed by the grave.

My Chitta Idamma had returned.

With hair all matted from not having bathed in months, skirt and blouse torn and fetid.

It was not just that she had returned with the same mutterings, laughter, and crazy talk. There was news within the news. Chitta was heavy with child, it seems!

Someone from the village had found her wandering about the city streets and had put her on a boat and had brought her here.

Not once had Pappa or I gone looking for Chitta, or tried to bring her back. Not just that, once when I went to the city for something, had I not seen her and come away pretending I hadn't? Pappa, who went to the city almost every other day, might have seen her a hundred times....

When the neighbours went over, they found Chitta sitting on the veranda, legs outstretched, picking lice from her hair and popping them into her mouth, and chewing with relish ...!

I heard about all this, but had not bothered to even pass that way. Jacintha and her mother kept saying things to comfort me, and had urged me to visit her.

When Ida Chitta came home, Pappa was not there. As for the karambi, she had left Pappa by then.

It was in the evening, when the church bell was ringing for prayer, that Pappa came to see the sight. He had already heard about her return from others. Some of the neighbours were still standing around in the courtyard. He scattered them with a spurt of vile abuse. Then, like one who was blind, he stepped across Chitta who sat at the doorway and went indoors.

It was dark inside. But there was no one in that house to light a tin lamp or a candle on the stand. When night fell, Chitta began to cry, and then to scream 'I'm hungryyy! I'm hungryyyy!' Pappa heard the loud wailing, but stayed put inside.

Hearing her cries, one of the neighbours brought Chitta some rice and curry. She attacked the food greedily, filling her enlarged belly in no time. Then she lay down on her side and slept like a baby.

On the third night too, I did not touch Jacintha, or talk to her. At midnight, when I rose from the mat, Jacintha was sleeping soundly.

With a burning candle in my left hand and that gold chaavi in my right, I wandered all over the house. When I finally got back to her, there she was, sitting up in bed. Waiting for me. Like an old woman who had come to mass before the church had opened!

I blew out the candle and tried to go back to sleep, as if nothing had happened. But, Jacintha stopped me.

She started talking to me about things, beginning with what she saw me do on our first night. All my defences were shattered. I confessed to her – as if to a priest in a confessional – the story of that chaavi which fumed inside me like a burning ember in the incense bowl.

You are mad, insane, she bawled angrily, urging me to throw that chaavi in the river. She then tried to take it from me by force, but I could not even imagine giving it to her. Somehow, I had come to believe that it was the chaavi that had kept me from going insane.

As I sat there like a wet rooster, holding that chaavi and staring into the dark, Jacintha told me a story. But, before that, she held my hand and led me to another room. She opened it with a rusty old key.

I had not failed to notice that door, which looked like it was never opened. The rusty hinges chirred as she struggled to open the old wooden door. Dust and a rank smell rushed into my nostrils. In the light of the kerosene lamp, I saw the old walls covered with cobwebs, the plaster crumbling off them. On the wall was a dusty, cobwebbed fuskya icon of Our Lady of Velankanni, festooned with red silk and brocade garlands.

From the ceiling hung an 'ever-burning' lamp that had run out of oil. Dusty, extinguished candles and incense sticks stood on a wooden stand before the icon. But it was not these that caught my attention.

It was an immense pit right in the centre of the room which occupied three fourths of its packed mud floor. So huge, you could hardly enter the room. All around the pit, sticky white earth lay in mounds. In the light of the kerosene lamp, I saw on them rat dung, remains of lizards and tiny holes made by ant-lions.

Jacintha began her story:

'Father had been a fervent devotee of Our Lady of Velankanni. Every year, he would visit the shrine during the festival. As was the custom, he would shave his head, rub turmeric on it, and bathe in the sea before returning.

Father would attend mass in the parish church and receive Holy Communion every day. He would reach the church before dawn. He would then go to the cupola of St. Anthony by the riverside and kneel before the idol of Our Lady for a long time, eyes closed in prayer. And so he had been, from the time I remember.

One morning, after his usual prayer, just as he was about to leave the cupola for mass, a lady appeared before him as if out of a bolt of lightning. Sheathed in a flowing, glittering, golden robe, waves of an unearthly light rippled all around her. She extended towards him a clay pot covered with red silk, and said: "Get back home before daybreak ... and make sure you give a share to the poor and the weak and the needy...." With that, the divine lady vanished, as suddenly as she had appeared.

Father felt as if he had been blinded. He had no idea how he reached home.

By the time he got back, father had forgotten the lady's instructions. Greed and selfishness awoke in him. Without telling even mother, he buried that pot in this floor. He had decided to take his time and remove its contents gradually.

When he tried to examine it a few days later, he found that the clay pot kept receding into the earth by itself. The more he dug, the deeper the pot sank into the earth. Further and further away from his reach.

Father forgot all about food and sleep and kept digging like a madman. He then sat still by the pit for a long time, his head in his hands. He wept and prayed before the icon of Our Lady to get the treasure back ... in vain.

One morning, he packed his bag, said goodbye to mother, and left home. Said, he was off to Velankanni. Before he left, he locked the room and gave the key to mother, saying: "No one should open this door."

If father found out that I had opened this room, he might even kill me. I was a child then, and barely remember what happened. Father now roams the church grounds at Velankanni, searching for someone. Or he sits in the church, as if waiting for someone.

Every year, mother goes to Velankanni to meet father, to invite him home. After he expressed a wish to see his daughter, she took me too, five or six times. Many people in the village have seen father at Velankanni. Some even tried to bring him back, but in vain.

Mother still keeps going to Velankanni, like someone visiting a grave for the annual memorial prayers....'

When I heard this story, I thought to myself: I too have heard these things before, although not in such detail. Perhaps, I might even have seen her father when I was a child, in the time before my memory....

Mamma Returns

It was the day after Ida Chitta returned. In the church, morning service was in progress. Raising the wine-filled casa with both hands, the vicar pronounced: 'This is the cup of My blood, the blood of the new and everlasting covenant; it will be shed for you and for all, for the forgiveness of sins. Do this in memory of Me....'

When that sentence ended, I, the sacristan, would ring the hand bell in a particular rhythm for a short spell. The faithful would kneel, palms together, and bow before the casa. They would raise their heads only when the bell fell silent.

The moment the ringing stopped, when the silence had reached its very peak, a loud cry pierced the church, sending a shudder through the gathering.

Running up to the altar with a cry came Ida Chitta, blood streaming from her. As the shocked people scrambled to their feet, their hands still together, I saw Pappa bounding up behind her, bloodied chopper in hand, and with a ferocity that seemed unstoppable.

Leaping up to Ida Chitta like a maniac, Pappa hacked furiously at her neck and stomach and chest. Chitta lay writhing in blood, crying, screaming, and then, grew still forever.

Even at that time, standing close by, I saw a faint but unmistakable heaving in Chitta's swollen belly.

Women and children scattered, shrieking loudly. The vicar and the others, not knowing what to do, shouted something at Pappa, but kept their distance.

Chopper in hand, Pappa turned and started walking towards Father Varghese, who still held the casa. Pappa's face at that moment was a sight to behold. The lone eye, the stubble, and the blood, all gave his expression a terrible severity.

The vicar and his flock trembled in fear. Who knew what Pappa had in mind? He still held the chopper, so people kept their distance.

The vicar did not move, trying not to show his fear. A priest, running scared in the middle of mass, in front of all these people.... It would have been such a shame ...!

But, what everyone feared did not happen. Pappa approached the vicar, and knelt at his feet. Fell to the ground face down, with a piercing wail.

The blood that had pooled by the altar slowly started to dry and cake. The priest moved back a little and tried to lift Pappa to his feet, but he didn't even raise his head.

As for me, I just stood there by the altar, bell in hand, not knowing what to do, not reacting in any way, not even shedding a single tear.

No one said anything to me. Nor I to them.

Like a candle that burned but would not melt, I stood there, aflame.

It took an hour for the police to arrive. Until then, both Pappa and Chitta lay there as they were. The policemen arrested Pappa and took him away, pushing and shoving him.

Pappa hung bent and withered, like a spinach plant that had had too much sun. Still, I saw a certain peace on his face. The peace that came from having fulfilled some great responsibility!

They took Ida Chitta away, wrapped and bound up in a reed mat. It was only by noon the next day, after the post-mortem, that Chitta was brought back to the house. In a coffin, dressed in a long white robe and shoes, and sprayed with perfumes and talcum powder.

When Chitta's funeral rites were being performed, it was the chemmador who did the sacristan's duties, even though I had offered to do it myself.

The body was kept in the churchyard, and mass conducted for the departed. Entering the cemetery for the burial, I noticed something. It was that same pregnant woman's grave from which I had got the gold chaavi years back that had now been dug open for Chitta.

Here in one pregnant woman's grave, was being buried another, her Achilles' tendon severed....

I stood by, recollecting the writings about death and funeral rites in Mammanji's book that I had read just hours before. When a death happened in the parish, whoever it was, Mammanji would rush there. She would be present throughout, handing out instructions and advice.

If it was a man, Mammanji would just pass on instructions. If it was a woman, she would lead the proceedings with the other widows.

In her notes, Mammanji had written, that among all the blessed deeds, the act of bathing and dressing the dead was the greatest.

It was said that the spirit did not leave the house and the surroundings for seven days after death. For this reason, the dead man's bed was to be placed outside the house for at least seven days, and no one was allowed to use it.

Even after the funeral, the table with the linen spread on it, the cross, the cathisal, and everything else were to be left exactly as they were. You had to make sure that the light never went out in the house and that the family ate no fish or meat and the like.

The dying were to be given 'chevittorma'. There was to be no loud crying immediately after the death, in case it unsettled the spirit.

One who had been ill meets death not like a lamp that is blown out by the wind. Instead, it happens as slowly as darkness overcomes day. Bit by bit.

In Mammanji's language, it was called 'the dissolution'.

Mammanji would look at those approaching death and pronounce thus: 'One eye is dead. The hand is dead. That man's feet were already dead yesterday....'

When, the very old – bent with age – die, their backs straighten out by themselves. If the eyes were open at death, they had to be pressed shut when still warm. And similarly, the mouth. The jaws had to be closed and tied. To keep the belly from swelling, salt crystals had to be sprinkled on it, or aloe rubbed on it. The dead were to be bathed in lukewarm water. It was good to stand them on their feet and pour water over their heads. Before that, the clothes and ornaments were to be removed, but not in a careless manner. On every occasion, there were prayers to be recited with devotion.

When the earrings are removed: 'The ear-ornaments that our Creator the Lord gave as alms to be worn on earth, we now remove from this daughter in Thy name', says the widow who leads the removal.

'Praise be Thine, Jesus', say the helpers in response.

When the wedding ring is removed: 'Lord, this sanctified wedding ring, a blessing from Thee to take part in the consecration of married life, we now remove from this daughter's fingers in Thy name'.

In this way, prayers were to be recited for every organ, after making the sign of the cross on each with water.

'If the eyes of Thy daughter have sinned by seeing that which was vexing to Thee, we now plead for Thy forgiveness.'

'Jesus, we beg Thy forgiveness.'

'If these ears have sinned by hearing that which was displeasing to Thee....'

'If these lips have spoken that which was ill and contrary to Thee....'

Thus, for every organ, the sign of the cross was to be made and prayed for. There were prayers to be said with each piece of clothing that was removed. Even the undergarments were to be put on in the correct way. To prevent bleeding from the vagina, a folded cloth had to be fixed in place.

At the time of death, stagnant dirt would stream from all human beings. It would have a particularly vile smell. Therefore, those parts need special cleaning. Men's faces were not to be rinsed while shaving; if rinsed, the skin too might come off....

The dead were to be dressed in their wedding clothes, which had to be preserved for this purpose.

It was common for the poor or the miserly to rent or borrow a wedding suit from someone who had got married recently. Mammanji would counsel them that however poor they were, women ought to wear their wedding dress of alleshum kuppayam or white gown, and men, suits, to the ceremony in church. These clothes had to have been specially stitched for them. After death, before the body was bathed and placed in the coffin, these very clothes were to be put on it.

And many things like that....

But my Chitta never got any of these cares or prayers owed to the departed. Was it not like an orphan that Chitta was....

My Pappa hacked Chitta and wounded her. The doctors cut her up. Those who put Chitta in the coffin broke her bones as she was all curled up. Not for a single night did they let her lie at home....

After Pappa's brothers and others in his family protested, it was decided that Chitta would not be buried in the family tomb.

On hearing the news, Mamma came home. Jacintha and mother-in-law and some of the nonas were wailing like Pulayas. Weeping and recounting memories of Chitta, Mamma turned our house into a house of death.

No one in my family approved of Mamma's return. There were frowns on every face. All of them ignored her. Everyone thought that Mamma would go back to Xavy after the funeral. But Mamma did not go back. Mamma had left Xavy for good.

Mamma walked confidently into the house bought in her name by selling her gold.

Mamma had become weak and thin and appeared a lot older than she was. How different she had looked when she had left with Xavy!

Mamma then and Mamma now were as different as a field where the grain was ripe, and one in which it had been reaped.

Mamma and I did not say a word to each other; we were still like in the old days.

One by one, people parted after the customary meal of rice served with lentils, curried gourd, and a large pappadam. In the end, only Mamma, Jacintha, and I were left in the house.

Mother-in-law left, murmuring about her cows.

Sometime in the night, we entered sleep, without sleeping.

Later, I learned that Xavy had not treated my Mamma as a wife at all; that they had not led a family life. Instead, Xavy had sold my Mamma. He had been making money by selling her to his friends. And others. Mamma had been waiting for a chance to get away from Xavy. Chitta's death turned out to be her escape route.

From the next day onwards, Mamma busied herself with the chores of the house. The day after Ida Chitta's seventh-day ceremony, Jacintha and I left for her house.

This much was true. Had Mamma not come back, that house, small and made of boards as it was, with no one living in it, would have fallen to the termites.

The Lost Chaavi and a Strange Dream

Three months after my wedding, when Jacintha was walking alone from the church to the cemetery after Sunday mass, Mamma approached her. Her manner was more familiar than usual. Lately, Mamma and Jacintha had started making small talk.

'No news for us yet, Mol?' asked Mamma in a hushed voice.

Jacintha's face brimmed over with sorrow.

She did not answer Mamma even after her prayers at the cemetery. Mamma kept asking her about it. Finally, she relented. With the burning candles and the numberless graves as witness, she shamefacedly told that truth which any woman would hesitate to tell a mother-in-law.

Mamma gave her a lot of advice, and before they parted, scolded her mildly: 'If a feast of a girl like you puts her mind to it, what's not possible, Mol?'

That year too, Achamma Chechi went to Velankanni. It was a Friday. That night, like always, I crossed myself on the forehead and all four edges of the mat and lay down to sleep.

When Jacintha came to sleep by my side, I noticed something unusual. She had had an oil bath, washed herself with perfumed soap, applied scented oils all over, and had worn her hair loose with jasmine flowers in it....

She did not put out the lamp. At the rustle of clothes, I opened my eyes. Only to see her standing next to me, without a stitch on her ...!

Like one who was dead, I tried to go back to sleep. But, before I could defend myself, she had commenced battle with the speed of a warrior on horseback. Before that, I was sure, she would have called out to all the saints and prayed and made offerings.

I lay on my back with my eyes shut, like a complete innocent. Sometime later, I wept in ecstasy. After it was all over, she got up, put her clothes on, and lay down as if nothing had happened.

Lying on her back, she recited three 'Our Father in Heaven's, three 'Hail Mary's, and three 'Praise be to the Trinity's, and offered them all to the saints.

After a while, very gently, even fearfully, she asked me: 'Shall we throw that chaavi away? It's for nothing that you're searching for its lock. Look at my father, wasting his life wandering around Velankanni ... why end up like that?'

I only grunted in response. A hope began to take shape in Jacintha. She kept murmuring about the absurdity of that chaavi into my ear.

I got up. Searched and found my mundu, which lay somewhere on the floor. Groped for its corner, loosened the gold chaavi from the knot and offered it to Jacintha.

Jacintha received it greedily and placed it safely under her pillow.

From then on, our nights continued this way. I never initiated anything. Nor did I resist. From that night, yes, it was from that unforgettable night that I began to see a strange dream.

Like all men, once it is over, the deep slumber that comes from battle fatigue would begin to overtake me from the very next moment. In that very instant, I would wake with a start upon seeing a dream.

Pork was an essential item in every house in the village during festivities, be it Christmas, Easter, or the parish festival. On all those days, I had seen pigs being killed. It had always aroused in me the feeling of a brutal celebration.

A large pit is dug in the middle of a vast, uninhabited compound. The pig to be killed is buried upside down in the pit, in such a way that only its anus is visible above the ground. By then, a curious crowd would have gathered, as if to watch fireworks.

In a short while, the pig's anus would dilate rapidly like the mouth of a volcano and explode with a loud blast, spraying the animal's intestines and filth all over ...

The difference between reality and my dream was that the pig in the dream had the face of a man. It was when the explosion happened that I would come awake with a start.

One such day, Johnacha, Pappa's younger brother and the current occupant of the tharavad, said to me: 'Mammanji had put it in writing that a share of the ancestral property must be given to Fransocha as well. So, here is something for you', he said, slipping a fat envelope of currency notes into my hand.

There was also that old rosewood chest of Mammanji. It was to go to Pappa. Perhaps Mammanji had written so because we were the ones maintaining the tradition of sacristans in the family.

The books Mammanji used, a rosary, a ventheenja with a heart-shaped casket containing holy relics hooked on to it, candle-stands, statuettes and portraits of the saints, a gold cross, sheets of paper containing Mammanji's notes, the pointy sappath that Mammanji used to wear on that special day, her kotheenja, slides for the hair, silver bangles and other ornaments, a large hat, thuni and kavaya, eyeglasses, a veil to drape over the head, a cloth purse ... there were many many such things in that chest.

Propping it up somehow, Sandhyavacha and three others brought that chest to Mamma's house that evening. They had to struggle to bring it inside through the narrow doorway of that small board house.

From what I heard, after bringing the chest indoors, Sandhyavacha left without saying a word to Mamma. Except for Jacintha, no one in the family would talk to Mamma.

Still, Mamma knew it was Joona Mammanji's chest. Mamma might have felt that the chest radiated the aura of some holy relic. And for that reason, she looked at it with great awe and reverence. Though the key to the chest was in its hole, Mamma did not even touch it.

Mamma went to the bathroom and bathed with great care, and put on a freshly washed saree and blouse. She lit candles and incense sticks before the fuskya icons on the stand. And then, invoking Mammanji silently, pleading forgiveness for all her lapses, and bowing before the chest in obeisance, she opened it gently.

Mamma inhaled deeply the divine and uncommon fragrance that flowed from it. That noble scent of a proud lineage took hold of her and possessed her completely.

Then, stripping off her saree, she took out Mammanji's thuni, silk kavaya and shoes, kotheenja and hat, silver needle and brooch, necklace, amulet, and ventheenja, and wore them all elegantly and in their proper order. Then she started examining the chest in detail.

Mamma had heard about the prayer – of miraculous power – that my Pappanji's Pappa had handed down in writing. That was what she was searching for.

Mamma found it.

In Mammanji's Holy Bible. The yellowed paper was so old that if it was not handled carefully, it would have turned to dust in her hands. Mamma recited it repeatedly, and with reverence. Initially, it was very difficult for Mamma to make out the words.

It was evening when I came to know that the chest had been taken to Mamma's house. I quickly rang the bell for prayer and left the church. I had not been to that house after Chitta's seventh-day ceremony. No one knew how Mamma was getting by there.

Many a time, I had seen Mamma in the church. Just seen, that's all. Jacintha would keep telling me that Mamma was not the same person anymore, that she had changed a lot. That I should visit her, talk to her, give her something, and so on.

I reached the house. The door was closed, but not latched. From between the boards, I could see the light of the kerosene lamp inside. I felt terribly anxious at the prospect of facing Mamma alone, so I peered through a gap in the door. The sight I saw ...!

My Joona Mammanji sat reading in the light of the kerosene lamp. The light had spread a glow on Mammanji's face, giving it an ethereal radiance ...!

A split second. I looked once again closely. No, I was mistaken. It was not Mammanji. It was Mamma. So completely absorbed was she in her reading that it had taken on all the glory and ardour of a ritual.

I did not have the strength to stay there any longer. Or, to look again. I went back to Jacintha. Without even having dinner, I lay down to sleep. When Jacintha tried to initiate our regular intercourse that night, for the first time, I discouraged her.

That night I did not see the usual dream of the killing of the pig that kept haunting my sleep. Perhaps for that reason, in the nights that followed too, I kept disappointing Jacintha.

Mamma Transformed

The first Friday of the month after the chest was brought home. That day, Mamma didn't wear her usual saree and blouse to church. Instead, she put on Mammanji's shiny thuni and kavaya and ornaments, and came to church with the same grandeur that Mammanji used to on that special day.

At first, the parishioners could not tell who this choochi was. They kept staring at Mamma. Then started asking each other. Those who knew Mamma, could tell once they looked more closely. Even I was taken aback, but then I remembered the sight I had seen.

On the first Fridays of every month, apart from mass, there would be special rites: the Adoration with the Holy Communion displayed in the reliquary, Lateenja in Latin, followed by Benediction. That day, there would be as many people in church as for Sunday mass.

Everyone in our family thought that their dead Juana Mammanji had been resurrected and had come to church.

Overnight, Mamma had lost her voluptuous manner and its alluring effect, and was transformed into a noble and serious-looking choochi.

After the service, Mamma went to the cemetery and prayed at Mammanji's tomb, for longer than usual. From the day she got that chest, Mamma had been reading Mammanji's writings with great devotion.

From the cemetery, Mamma went straight to the riverside. She then immersed herself fully at the same spot Mammanji used to on those special days, and stepped on to the bank dripping wet. Clicking her fingers in that same rhythm, singing that song, which no one else knew, in that same tune, and with the same dance-like steps, she walked home.

All those who stood watching, followed Mamma home. By the time she reached the house, a fair crowd had accompanied her there. Among them were the same relatives who had hated and shunned her. All of them stood piously, palms together.

Mamma gave them blessed ventheenjas. Scolded some of them. Foretold the future of a few.

As all this was completely unexpected, everyone regretted not having prepared any special dishes.

As soon as she had heard the news, Jacintha ran to Mamma's place. Then and there, Mamma said something about Jacintha that she herself did not know. A prediction which surprised everyone. Jacintha was going to be a mother ...!

That day, when Jacintha told me this, what I recalled was Mammanji's notes about pregnancy.

Since then, on the first Friday of every month, Mamma has been entering this extraordinary state.

And how many successful predictions she had made, like the one about Jacintha's pregnancy.

Mamma now gives consecrated waist-cords to the childless. Provides medicines. Exorcises evil spirits. How quickly people started coming to Mamma; to get jobs, to stop family quarrels, to keep husbands from drinking. Kosamma aunty, who had been married off, now comes to Mamma the first Friday of every month.

Of late, people of other religions, and from surrounding villages too, have started to visit Mamma.

What made Mamma different from Mammanji was that Mammanji had never taken anything from anyone. Mamma though, takes gifts and money from visitors.

Rich devotees even give her large donations. Mamma distributes herbal nostrums for many more ills than Mammanji had.

All this is from hearsay. How many first Fridays have come and gone! I alone was yet to visit Mamma.

From the time I heard that Jacintha was pregnant, I had been seeing that dream and coming awake with a start, without even having had intercourse. And for that reason, I would not go to Jacintha's house often. I started taking my meals at the vicar's or at teashops.

Mine is a meagre diet. The feed of a sparrow was all I needed.

Of late, the recurrent dream had become more and more detailed.

Not too far from the compound where the pig was killed, in the background loomed a large church painted white, its great spires rising way up into the sky. Soon after, like witnesses to the killing, there started to appear a clergyman dressed for Holy Mass, altar boys in oppa and moosha, and boys swinging caskets of burning incense.

Sometimes, I would hear all three bells ringing together, as when the reliquary is raised during the Benediction that follows the Adoration.

With each night that passed, the dream became more detailed, and its horror, greater. Sleep, for me, had turned into a torment.

That was how I started to think about that gold chaavi again. And whenever I did, I would feel a terrible sense of loss.

Once, when I was startled awake upon seeing that same dream, I felt an urge to take back that chaavi immediately.

The clock on the wall showed twelve midnight. A pregnant Jacintha was sleeping soundly. I remembered Mammanji's saying that pregnant women should not be called in their sleep. But still, I woke Jacintha. In the light of the ever-burning lamp hung before the fuskya icons, I saw how startled she was. She was drenched in sweat. I asked her to return that gold chaavi to me.

Though she had decided to throw it away, Jacintha had had doubts when she noticed its shine. She had given it to her mother, who, on grinding it, found that it was indeed gold. She had then secretly sold it to a goldsmith she knew, for cash!

When I heard this, my heart churned violently. That very moment, I rose from the mat, put on a shirt and walked out into the dark.

Sobbing, Jacintha tried to stop me, but I paid no attention. At that late hour, I went to the church verandah and slept there, and suffered no nightmares.

Ever since, I stopped going to Jacintha as well. With the permission of the vicar, I would eat and sleep in the kuseenja.

Jacintha and mother-in-law visited me several times to try and take me home, but I refused to go with them. Nor could all the counsels of the vicar and the parishioners make me change my mind.

One morning, I came to know that Jacintha had had a baby boy. As usual, after ringing the prayer bell, I was on my way to the riverside to squat there. My godfather Lasaracha too came there regularly, before it was light. He had to pass Jacintha's house on his way to the riverside, and it was mother-in-law who told him the news and asked that I be informed.

The birth had taken place that very morning. It happened at home and it was Mamma who had served as midwife.

Like Mammanji used to do, Mamma had now started to assist at births and in the bathing and preparing of the dead for burial, even though she was not a widow.

'They said, the baby looks like you.'

I knew very well that godfather had said all this knowing how I would respond.

That very day, mother-in-law paid for someone's bus fare to go to Velankanni and inform Thummi Chettan that he had become a grandfather. She and Jacintha were hoping that at least on this occasion, their husbands would have a change of heart and return.

They had got it wrong. We were wandering in our own worlds, like two sleepwalkers.

The boy who brought milk to the church every day also brought news of home. I have never asked him anything, but he would tell me everything.

Mammanji Among the Saints

Time, like beads on a rosary, slipped by all too quickly.

When she started getting a lot of money as offerings and donations, Mamma had the old board-shack demolished and built a solid stone and mortar house in its place. In just six or seven months, even the whitewashing was done and she had moved in.

Everyone considered this a blessing from Mammanji. Where could Mamma have got the power to go about more energetically than a man, and to lead everything and everyone!

The entire family turned up for the housewarming ceremony.

For the first time since I had grown up, Mamma came to me. Talked to me. Insisted that I come for the benediction of the house and the feast afterwards, that I should forget about the past and take part in all the ceremonies.

In the new house, next to the fuskya icons of the Sacred Heart, the Virgin Mother and St. Sebastian, hung an enlarged portrait of Mammanji, adorned by a brocade garland. On a wooden stand below Mammanji's portrait were placed the candle stand, the ever-burning lamp, the Bible, and other things that Mammanji had used.

All this is hearsay, because I did not attend the housewarming, though the vicar had insisted I should. It was my duty as sacristan to accompany him with the candles and holy water for the benediction. But that day, the chemmador went in my place. I had sneaked off to the city.

One day, a telegram came from the jail. Pappa was very ill. Those concerned were to reach him immediately, it said.

The telegram had come to Mamma. Mamma ran to inform Johnacha. Sandhyavacha and Louisacha set off immediately. They did not ask or tell me anything. Like everything else, I came to know this from the boy who brought the milk.

Just a month back, Mamma had visited the jail and met Pappa as he served his sentence. At first, Pappa refused to pay attention to Mamma or even to look at her. It was only recently that things had started to change slightly.

As he had lost his way, was not needed by any one, and had lived as a menace to all, no one had tried to get

Pappa released on bail, or to fight his case. They said that it would have been futile even if they had tried. After all, the evidence was so strong against him.

That day there was no news of those who had gone to the jail to make enquiries. But, the next evening, a *machuva* docked at the church-landing. Fitted with long oars on either side, it was rowed by Kamaru Ikka, Pappa's dear friend.

I was seated at the foot of the flagmast by the church-landing, thinking about that lost chaavi, when I saw a coffin laid across the machuva's seats. On either side of the coffin sat Sandhyavacha and Loiusacha, their hands resting on it.

I did not understand anything at first. The two younger uncles were bringing a coffin in a machuva. Had they not gone to find out about Pappa?

Louisacha got off from the machuva with a grave expression and strode away rapidly. They saw me, but said nothing.

In a short while, Louisacha, accompanied by Alsocha, Visenthiyacha, Lasaracha, Johnacha, and others, came rushing back to the riverside. Following them, Mamma, mother-in-law, and some women came running, wailing loudly.

As I stood dazed beneath the flagmast – like a flagmast myself – Mamma came and hugged me, crying.

She kept saying over and over again, 'Your Pappa's gone, Mon ... your Pappa's gone....'

Mamma's unexpected touch made me terribly uneasy. As if I could not bear contact with another body. I wriggled out of those arms in a way no one would notice.

Those who had assembled lifted the coffin off the machuva and set it on the ground. Later, as we walked home, someone kept ringing the death-knell in the order of one-two, one-two....

The bells I that ought to ring, were now being rung by someone else, even when I was present.

Hearing the news, more people arrived. Someone put his hand on my shoulder and led me home behind the coffin. I had no choice but to go with them. Someone had fetched from the church the cathisal and the silver cross to be placed at the head of the coffin.

The coffin in which Pappa lay was placed on a table in the living room of Mamma's new house. They had put Pappa in the coffin after the post-mortem, and one could barely see his face. White bandage wrapped around the head, white cotton in the nostrils, black coat and trousers.

The odour of incense-sticks and a sharp-smelling perfume filled the air.

Pappa's face looked as if it had been painted yellow. He had died of severe jaundice. We had received no news of his illness. It was only when the disease had reached its last stage, and Pappa was dying, that the jail authorities realized he had jaundice.

No matter how severe it was, jaundice could be cured with just three days of treatment using a herbal preparation known to my Mammanji, and now to Mamma. It called for little expense or effort; on how many patients was Mamma using it effectively, to this day!

Just for this purpose, Mamma had planted castor saplings in the yard and tended them carefully. And to think Pappa had to die of jaundice....

It was then that I saw Mamma's new house. My own house seemed like a stranger's house to me.

It was decided that Pappa would be buried in the family tomb where Pappanji and Mammanji were buried. As he had died a day before, and the post-mortem had already been done, the burial could not wait much longer. Like Ida Chitta, Pappa too did not receive any of the attentions prescribed for a dead. It was decided to place the body in the tomb by seven in the evening. Two Petromax lanterns were readied for this.

Only once in my life had I seen a funeral conducted after dark – that of a baby, dead at birth.

The scene of a funeral conducted after dark, in the faint light of lanterns, arouses a strange terror in us. The voices and the lights disturb the deep slumber

of a cemetery lying immersed in darkness and silence.
The monstrous shadows of tombstones and crosses and
bushes. And even as a grave is filled with light, the dense
darkness that crowds all around it like a pack of vultures
waiting to devour their prey!

It was around five in the afternoon that the gravedigger
and the mason broke open the family tomb. All they had
to do was to remove the three concrete slabs with shiny
black tiles on them, and clean the cemented pit below.
Moving the concrete slabs aside with a crowbar, they
saw a coffin that had lost its coat of varnish, but was
hardly damaged otherwise.

The grave digger got down in to the pit and opened
the coffin. He nearly fainted at what he saw.

Mammanji's body lay there in the exact state it
had been in when she was buried! Her face serene and
beautiful, and still rosy-cheeked ...! The long, shiny white
robe she had been dressed in that day, the wreath on her
head, the black cross in her hands; all of it intact. The
flowers, the roses included, looked as if they had been
freshly plucked. From the time the coffin was opened, a
sweet, celestial fragrance flowed from it.

They immediately informed the vicar, who came
running to the cemetery. He looked at Mammanji's
face and said that it had an unearthly and divine glow.
Such grace was to be found only on the holy faces of the

saints. The vicar got down into the grave and examined the coffin, clothes, and flowers. This is a great miracle, he exclaimed.

He sent one of the church wardens to inform the bishop at his manor. On the vicar's instructions, someone kept ringing the church bell continuously.

Hearing the news, parishioners and people of all communities streamed into the cemetery. Once it reached us, all those who sat around Pappa's body – except for me, Mamma, Kosamma Auntie, Jacintha, and my mother-in-law – ran to the cemetery.

Those who had seen Mammanji's body on the day she died, now retrieved that image from their greying memories and compared it to the figure that lay in the coffin. Yes, how Juana choochi's face had looked the day she was buried, it looked exactly the same now, they declared in one voice.

Everyone who rushed there, knelt before Mammanji's tomb, lit candles, threw flowers, said prayers. The countless candles burning around the tomb lit it up like a bonfire. The cemetery reverberated with songs of prayer.

Following the vicar's instructions, another grave was dug and Pappa was buried in it. Since Pappa's burial was attended by everyone who had come to see Mammanji, it turned out to be the biggest funeral ceremony the parish had ever seen. Pappa got the prayers of a great many people.

It was past nine at night when Pappa's funeral ended.

It was when we came to the cemetery with Pappa's body that *we* saw Mammanji. We were like those struck by lightning. A living face, Mammanji's ...!

I was twelve years old when Mammanji died. To this day, that face is clear in my memory.

The small burial mound that was made over Pappa's grave after it was filled was soon flattened by the stampeding crowds. People forgot Pappa like the mass they had seen the day before. Mammanji stole even Mamma's and my attention.

None of the parishioners slept that night. The vicar too stayed on in the cemetery. To protect Mammanji's tomb from rain and sunlight, that very night they erected a large bamboo and tarpaulin shed above it. It was then covered with white cloth and decorated with tender palm leaves and flowers. Four Petromax lanterns burned all night.

During the mass the next morning, the vicar requested everyone not to throw flowers on the body. He was afraid that if flowers were offered at this rate, they would fill the grave in just a day!

By morning, people started arriving from neighbouring villages as well. Newspapers sent their reporters and photographers.

At around eleven-thirty in the morning, the bishop arrived at the cemetery, having postponed all his other programmes. On his request, the coffin with the body in it was lifted out of the grave.

The bishop examined Mammanji's hair and nails. They had as much, or indeed, even more life in them than when she was buried; that was the bishop's verdict.

The bishop raised his eyes towards the sky, crossed himself on the forehead, knelt, and conducted all sorts of prayers. Then he asked for the coffin to be closed and put back in the tomb for now. He then instructed us that the tomb should not be opened for anyone else.

The parishioners stood around in groups, discussing how the bishop would now send a report to the Pope, and might soon initiate procedures for Mammanji's sainthood.

Even at that time, the news kept drawing crowds from neighbouring villages.

I have heard the story of a man who had died a sinner, whose body was found intact years later when the grave was dug to bury someone else. After they sighted his fingernails, which kept growing like plantain leaves, and his hair, which grew like the numberless roots of a large tree, it was concluded that he had indeed been a sinner. A strange pallor had turned his face and limbs white.

Parishioners, and people of all communities who had come from wherever the fame had spread, started taking soil and candles and flowers from Mammanji's tomb. Conceiving them to be holy remains, they began installing them in their homes.

Tales of miracles, and colourful stories about Mammanji herself, both true and false, started spreading in the village and elsewhere. I also came to know that some people were making a lot of money by selling small prints of Mammanji's photographs copied from the portraits at home and at the tharavad.

After I left the house accompanying Pappa's body, I never went back again.

Pappa's seventh-day ceremony was held on the fifth day after the funeral. I attended the ceremony at the church, and though they insisted that I come home, I refused.

A Feverish Climax

On the first Friday of the month after they opened Mammanji's tomb, a crowd so large had gathered to see Mamma as if for the finale of the church festival.

Offerings in hand, ventheenjas around their necks, and prayers on their lips, the devotees kept flocking there. The atmosphere was heavy with the fumes and fragrance of incense.

Everyone had got together and had prepared a large spread on the table, and set plantain leaves on the floor.

After prayers at Mammanji's tomb, with all the usual preparations, Mamma walked to the river.

I don't know why I came to the riverside at that time. Normally, knowing Mamma would be coming there soon, I would have stayed away, somewhere out of Mamma's sight.

As I stood beneath the flagmast, my mind suddenly got tangled on the thought of that lost gold chaavi. And suddenly, like the rasp of spicy food that burns its way up to the forehead, like a whirlwind, like a bolt of lightning, the thought of that chaavi surged through my nerves.

Fire erupted in my head.

Like an epileptic, I lay writhing on the dry grass around the flagmast, limbs thrashing about. My eyes flipped backwards. Teeth gnashed together. Foam poured out of my mouth.

Everyone's attention turned from Mamma, who had come fully prepared for her dip in the river, towards me. Mamma too saw me in that state, and came running up to me. Gathering me in her arms and clasping my face to herself, she asked anxiously, 'Osha! Osha Mon ... what happened?'

She then turned around and ran to the river, and returned with water cupped in her palms. She sprinkled it on me, and then washed my face. She shook and called me as I lay there, as if unconscious. And then, quite effortlessly, she lifted me off that dry grass in her arms, and walked home.

Dressed the way Mamma was, and with me held me aloft in her arms, it must have been quite a spectacle.

Mamma was about to enter the house, her journey from the riverside over. Those who had expected Mamma to come there after her dip in the river, clicking her fingers, singing and dancing and showering blessings on everyone, were shocked by this sight.

'What happened to Osha?' They asked each other.

They wondered, from where, Mamma, at her age, had found the strength to carry a young man like me and walk this distance.

Mamma sat on the front verandah and laid me across her lap. The scene resembled that of Mother Mary cradling the body of Jesus after it was removed from the cross. At that moment, Mamma's sorrowful eyes were moist.

All those who had gathered, came closer. Made enquiries, gave attentions....

They took me from Mamma's lap and laid me down on a mat spread on the bed. Sprinkled water on my face again. Fanned me. Called my name repeatedly.

I heard everything. Knew everything. And as I'd kept my eyes open throughout, saw everything as well. I had only lost my ability to move, and to respond.

Mamma and our relatives took me to the hospital in the city. However much they tried, the doctors who examined me were unable to figure out what was wrong with me, or what had happened to me.

After conducting all kinds of tests, the doctors gave their verdict: there was nothing wrong with me physically. I was not ill. I was fully conscious. I could even think normally. A restful, waking sleep, that was all....

A week later, after prescribing some medicines for the sake of it, they said I could be taken home.

Not just on that Friday, but on none of the first Fridays of the months that followed could Mamma reach that peculiar state again. Nor did she try. Was Mamma deliberately putting an end to it all ...?

That very day, Jacintha came to me with the child and started nursing me with great care. She never went back home after that. It is the juices and the liquids that Jacintha pours into my mouth that keep me alive.

I urinate and defecate in this same position. Jacintha cleans everything without complaining. On every alternate day, she soaks a towel in lukewarm water and, turning me around, cleans me all over. It is now almost a month since I have been in this state.

It was on a Friday that a man walked into Jacintha's house, surprising everyone.

Soiled clothes, greying beard, cracked feet in sandals that had worn thin; these marked him out. It seems at first even mother-in-law did not recognize him!

It was Thummi Chettan, my father-in-law. For the life of her, she couldn't believe that he had finally returned from Velankanni. She hugged him and wept, holding him tight. Like in some movies.

Father got rid of his beard the very day he arrived. Cut his hair and clipped his moustache. Rubbed oil all over and bathed elaborately. Put on a white muslin shirt and mundu, freshly washed and neatly pressed with the coal iron-box.

When he returned from church after mass next morning, father-in-law opened that room that had been shut for years, and filled with raw earth the pit he himself had dug. He then brought crushed laterite and beat it on to the floor using a floor-leveller. Brought fresh dung from the cowshed, and mixing it with water, glazed the entire floor with it. Dusted and cleaned the walls and the ceiling. He then cleaned the dusty icon of Our Lady, and brought it into the living room.

It was the next day – that is, the third day after he arrived – that he came to see me.

It was only when she heard about her father's arrival that Jacintha left my side with the child. She returned the same day.

It was from the conversations between mother-in-law and Jacintha and Mamma that I learned about father-in-law's arrival; and in the same way too, about the filling of the pit and other things.

Father-in-law came into the room where I lay. Rather, the room where they had laid me. He stood very close to my bed.

Jacintha called out to me loudly, crying. Shook me, saying, get up, Father has come.

How the loved ones of the deceased would wail when people arrived to see the corpse dressed for burial ... that was the effect the scene had on me and the others.

They described me to father-in-law in detail, telling him about the nature of my condition and how I had had it from the time I collapsed in an attack of fits....

Father turned to Mammanji's portrait and prayed. He then asked them the truth about everything he had heard about Mammanji's miracles in Velankanni. Whenever they spoke of Mammanji, they all spoke with a thousand tongues.

The talk once again turned to me.

Like never before, I felt an intense urge to leap upright. To take Father along with me to some deserted place and ask him, tell him, about all sorts of things.

I had never felt that way with anyone else. It seemed to me that perhaps he might have had a great many things to tell me – just me – things only I would have understood. If he had such a wish, then should the others not arrange an opportunity for it....

I tried to jump to my feet....

But as always, like from the time I could remember, I lay there motionless like one who was not conscious. Not knowing for how much longer....

Glossary

Names

Also (pronounced Ul-so)	Aloysius
Caspar/Caipar	Caspar
Franso	Francis
Juana/Joona	Juana
Lasar	Lazarus
Josy/Osha	Joseph
Sandhyavu	Santiago
Thummi	Thomas
Varghese	George; from the Greek 'Georgios'
Visenthi	Vincent
Xavy	Xavier

Rituals

Achilles' tendon
   severed
                    It is believed that when pregnant women die, their spirits remain to haunt people. The Achilles' tendon is cut so as to cause the spirit to limp, and thus render it harmless.

Adoration
                    A Catholic rite; 'worship given to God alone'

all three bells
                    When all three types of bells in the church – the large one in the tower (here hung from a tree), a smaller one usually hung in the veranda, and the hand bell – are rung simultaneously to mark a special occasion during rites

Anatha
                    Prayer service for the departed, to be recited by the priest in church

Benediction
                    The part of the service in which the Congregation is blessed with the Blessed Sacrament; that is the Host and Eucharistic wine, which represents the Body and Blood of Christ

chevittorma	The deathbed ritual wherein the words 'Eesho-Mariyam-Ouseppe' (Jesus-Mary-Joseph) are chanted in the ears of the dying, in the belief that this will prevent impure thoughts from entering their minds at the hour of their passing
kombreria	A gathering to celebrate a feast; from the Portuguese *confraria*, meaning congregation
Devastha	A ritual during Lent wherein a group of volunteers walk all over the parish late at night, exhorting people to pray, stopping periodically to kneel and pray loudly to chase away evil spirits; from the Latin *devotio*, meaning 'devotion'
esthi	Conventions to be followed while attending rituals; from the Portuguese *esteio* meaning 'support'
Laudatha	*Laudate Dominum* ('Praise the Lord'), the opening words, in Latin, of Psalm 117. The shortest Psalm, it has been set to music by a number of composers, including Mozart. In

	India, it is sung at Catholic weddings along the western coast.
Lateenja	Litany; from the Portuguese *ladainha*
oppees	Obsequy, or a funeral or commemorative rite, usually performed at the grave; from the Latin *obsequiae*.
Pesaha	Easter or the paschal season; from the Hebrew *Pesach*, referring to the Jewish Passover festival. Pesaha also refers to Maundy Thursday.
seventh-day memorial	Mass conducted as a memorial to the dead on the seventh day of demise, usually followed by a feast. This is repeated on the 30th and 42nd day of demise
vespera	Vespers; the sunset prayer service, usually held on holy feasts or festivals; from the Latin *vespera*, meaning 'evening prayer'

Miscellaneous

acha	Brother; also used to address elders in general

alleshum kuppayam	Traditional wedding dress for Paranki women; long-sleeved blouse with loop closures rather than hooks
casa	Chalice, or the cup used to hold communion wine; from the Portuguese *casa*, meaning 'house'
cathisal	A type of candle stand used in churches, from where it is occasionally brought to homes for special rituals
chaavi	Key; from the Portuguese *chave*
chemmador	The church courier or messenger
choochi	Corruption of 'susi' (sister); a general term for Paranki women
Jooda Kazhuvery	'Jooda' means Jew, and here refers to Jesus' Jewish birth. 'Kazhuvery' is a word of abuse, which literally means a criminal condemned to death by hanging
kunjathas and kunjathos ...	From the Portuguese: *kunjatha* (*cunhada*, 'sister-in-law'), *kunjatho* (*cunhado*, 'brother-in-law'), *kumbari* (*compadre*, the name by which a child's godfather is referred to by

its parents), *kumbarichi* (*comadre*, godmother), *peelas* (*afilhado*, 'godchild'). *Nona* is 'lady' and *susi* is 'sister'.

kuseenja

From the Portuguese *cozinha*, for 'kitchen; here it refers specifically to the vicarage kitchen

ever-burning lamp

The 'eternal flame'; a lamp placed before icons – especially in church – which is never put out, supposedly following prescriptions in the Bible. Here it refers to a humbler version used in village homes, which are tin lamps made by hand, but for which they nevertheless use coconut oil rather than the cheaper kerosene.

fuskya icons

Religious icons framed in wood and glass; from the Latin *fascia*, meaning 'band' or 'girdle'

Ikka

Literally, 'elder brother'; used mostly among or to refer to Muslims

Kappiri Muthappans

Literally, 'Black Gods'; refers to the spirits of African slaves slain by the colonial Portuguese, who are worshipped as deities by Parankis and the coastal people. The Portuguese rulers of Kochi were forced to flee after their defeat at the hands of the Dutch in 1653. It is believed that they ritually murdered their most loyal slaves so that their spirits would faithfully guard their masters' treasures till they returned. To this day, 'sightings' of Kappiri Muthappans happen in Kochi. The 'cassava' reference is significant, since the tuber – now a staple – was first brought to these shores by the Portuguese from South America, along with cashew and jackfruit, among others. Hence the local name *kappa*, which derives from *kappal kizhangu*, literally 'tuber from the ship'.

Karambi   Literally 'black woman'; here refers to a 'low-caste' woman

kottodi   A strong local drink; literally 'mallet' – guaranteed to knock you out

machuva   A type of large row-boat that used to be the common means for ferrying people and goods on the Kochi coast

oppa and moosha   The white sleeveless mantle and the embroidered mantle worn on top of it by the altar boys who assist the priest during mass

Our Lady of
  Velankanni   The Virgin Mary; here referring to the deity at the famous sea-side shrine at Velankanni in Tamil Nadu

Paranki   Originally referring to the Portuguese, and later their descendants and dependents, including some communities they converted to Christianity; derived from 'Firangi', a common Eastern term for Europeans, believed to be derived from 'Franks'

Puthenpaana   A set of popular religious works, created mostly by European missionaries. For example, the German Jesuit grammarian Arnos Padre wrote the *Puthenpaana*, which re-tells the life of Jesus in the paana form of traditional Hindu devotional poetry. Chapters from it are recited at homes on special occasions – the chapter that deals with The Passion is recited on Good Friday, and so on. Apart from the Holy Bible, these were the only books to be read in coastal Christan homes in Kochi.

rathaal

A sort of ornamental showcase next to the altar in church where icons and idols are kept; from the Portuguese *retalho*, literally 'patch'

reliquary

Container for sacraments; from the Latin word *reliquiarium*

rope-fishing

Fishing using the Chinese fishing nets, said to have been introduced by visiting Chinese traders 600 years ago. The nets are attached to a platform erected on stilts and are controlled by thick ropes.

sacristan

An officer of the church, usually a layperson, who looks after church's property and assists the vicar in rituals; from the Latin *sacristanus*, meaning 'custodian of sacred objects'. The Catholic equivalent of the Protestant sexton, the post of sacristan is traditionally passed on from one generation to the next within the same family.

sacristy	Room for keeping vestments, sacred vessels, and church furnishings
Saint of Arthungal	Arthungal Veluthachan; literally 'The white father of Arthungal', originally a reference to a Portuguese missionary who was based there, but now identifying St. Sebastian, the patron saint of the church
sanku	Cloth used to wipe the chalice; from the Portuguese *sangue*, literally 'blood'
sappath	From the Portuguese *sapato*, meaning 'shoe'
tharavad	Denotes both the ancestral house and the joint family system that it was home to
thochas	A type of tall candle-stand used in churches; from the Portuguese *tocha*, literally 'torch'
vasi	Bowls; from the Portuguese *bacia*, meaning 'basin' or 'bowl'
venthosas	A type of flower vase used in altars; from the Portuguese *ventosa*, literally 'suction cup'

... wailing like	
Pulayas	Hired village mourners who usually belong to the lowly Pulaya community
yakshis	Female spirits believed to be seductive and malign

About the Author and the Translator

Author

JOHNY MIRANDA is an artist and writer of Malayalam fiction who lives in Kochi, Kerala. He has published a collection of novellas, *Vishuddhalikhitangal* (Holy Inscriptions) and a short novel *Jeevichirikkunnavarkku Vendiyulla Oppees* (*Requiem for the Living*). His works appeared in leading Malayalam magazines before they were published in book form. He works for the Kerala State Electricity Board, and lives with wife Blessy and daughters Clara and Celine in Kochi. He has also worked as a commercial artist in the same city.

Translator

SAJAI JOSE was born in Kochi and grew up in Kottayam, Kerala. He is a journalist and former copywriter, and currently works for an advertising agency in Bangalore. *Requiem for the Living* is his first published work of translation.